Brian C. McCullough

LIGHT *and* STONE

Fantasy Engineering
Colorado Springs, Colorado / Sultan, Washington

First edition

ISBN: 978-0-692-09806-6

TABLE OF CONTENTS

ACKNOWLEDGMENTS

This novel is a product of National Novel Writing Month 2017. For more information about this program, visit *http://www.nanowrimo.org*.

The hand model for the front cover photograph was Julie Heffner.

The photograph was created on February 15, 2018 using Kodak T-MAX 100 film, which was then processed and scanned by Moonphoto, Seattle, Washington (*http://www.moonphotolab.com*).

Heartfelt thanks to Kimberly and Anya for their patient support (and for not killing me during the initial month of writing).

AUTHOR'S NOTE

Due to the political and social changes of late 2017 and immediately afterward, some thematic elements in this novel may cause concern to some readers. My hope is that the context in which these elements are presented, along with the overall design of the story, will quickly make it clear that it was not my original intent to cause offense.

However, for anyone who would like additional information on the decisions I made about what to include in the novel, I have posted a brief summary online. To read it, please visit *http://lns-comments.blogspot.com*. (Please note, however, that the summary necessarily includes spoilers.)

—*Brian C. McCullough, March 2018*

PROLOGUE

Sunlight was everywhere.

In the cities and towns, people emerged from their houses and apartments, from their parkas and jackets, and they stretched and breathed deeply. In the schools and colleges, they grew absentminded and dreamed of summer.

On a wide stretch of meadowland in the middle of the American Inner West, blades of wild grass punched their way through the crumbly, dry ground. Under the hard blue sky, they forced aside the decayed shells of their past and stretched thin, fragile fingers toward the returning sun, grasping for life. Around and among them were tiny pinpricks of color, the wildflowers that defied the genocide of last summer's heat to make their mythological return from the netherworld, as they did every year. In the distance, a haze of fresh green haloed mute red terraces.

It was May, and the world was awakening.

ONE

It was hard for Jan to concentrate. Not only would she rather have been just about anywhere else than here—slogging through one of the last Art History classes of her last freshman month—but Fred Lopez, the instructor, had the nasty habit of leaving the classroom door wide open on clear days. Presumably he did this to keep himself from nodding off alongside his students as they all plodded through the endless procession of names and dates and movements and countermovements and scandals and disputes and images and shapes and colors. However, the open door had the unpleasant side effect of reminding them all of the delights that lay outside the classroom: fresh air tinged with new flowers, eucalyptus, and the nearby ocean, people laughing and chattering in the distance, and warm sun—at least until the fog rolled in again.

Jan fought to stay engaged, writing down everything Fred was saying in an attempt to force it into her head, but she kept wandering off. She caught herself wondering how much hell her mother was going to give her when she finally went home, or considering whether she should date someone, or whether she even cared about that.

At one point, she even noticed herself starting to plan out her sophomore year. How sure was she that she wanted to focus on graphic design, as she kept insisting in public? Or would she rather try for an actual art degree? And what if she switched to photography? She smiled a little at the thought of her mom blowing every gasket in her head, as she would surely do at such a suggestion.

But suddenly, in a neck-snapping stroke of coincidence, Jan found herself whipsawed back to the present by a name out of Fred's interminable list of names.

J. W. Wheeler.

Fred was sitting on the corner of his desk as he often did during lectures, his dark hair a bit ruffled, gesturing with a stainless steel pen in his right hand at an image being projected on the screen behind him.

"Now as you know—or at least you do if you've been paying attention the last few weeks—black-and-white art photography had pretty much petered out by the early Seventies. There were plenty of prints in museums and individual collections, but most people were convinced that black-and-white film was obsolete. Most new work at that point was being done on color transparency film, and that was being driven by the fashion and journalism markets.

"But a funny thing happened in 1979. A print of Ansel Adams' *Moonrise, Hernandez, New Mexico, 1941* sold at auction for twenty-two *thousand* dollars."

There was a murmur from the students; Fred continued. "It was the highest price ever paid for any photograph up until that time, and it was even more surprising considering that Adams had been cranking out prints of this particular photograph for years.

"Well, that changed the direction of the art. Young photographers went scrambling back to learn about the Zone System, which the preceding generation had pretty much ridiculed into the ground, and started working in black and white again. Meanwhile, collectors and dealers started rummaging through the back catalog to see what other sources of profit they could dig up. There was a lot of new interest in other old names, and people started driving up prices on all the Westons and the Strands and the Stieglitzes. Suddenly people knew who Ruth Bernhard and Imogen Cunningham were. Fifty years after they took their bold stand against the establishment, Group *f*/64 *were* the establishment. Brave forests gave their lives to make this country safe for a new generation of coffee-table books."

Fred pushed his horn-rimmed glasses back up onto the bridge of his nose and grinned. "Okay, maybe not. But the collectors and the dealers kept digging.

"And that brings us back to J.W. Wheeler."

Jan leaned forward. Fred clicked a button on the remote in his left hand, and the widely-known contours of *Moonrise* disappeared. In their place was a simple farmyard, utterly prosaic and yet full of telling details.

"Now the thing about Wheeler is that he's kind of a mystery," Fred continued. "He was a few years younger than the Group *f*/64 people, but he lived here in the Bay Area at the same time they were still practicing here, so he probably crossed paths with some of them. If so, he may have pissed them off.

"He kept doing a few things that would have been associated with pictorialism—the Great Satan of Group *f*/64 and the other modernists—such as allowing some elements to go out of focus. But the people who are tracking his prints down now talk about the sense of humanity in his work.

"This photograph behind me is called *Barnyard, Modesto, 1945*. Typical title for the time and place: no interpretation, no poetry—just a subject, a location, and a date. And at first glance, the photo doesn't seem particularly dramatic. But take a good, close look. There's nothing in the scene that's free of wear. All the tools have clearly been used for years and years. They all tell a story. And even though the far background is defocused, all of the technical aspects of the print show a deft hand and a master's touch.

"Wheeler practiced in San Francisco for a few years, he had a handful of shows, and then he suddenly vanished without a trace. So there aren't that many Wheeler prints out there, which means the prices are going up pretty quick. But no one can tell him, because no one can find out where he is or if he's still alive."

Fred glanced over to the clock next to the screen, then clicked the remote again. The image disappeared. "All right! Finals prep next Tuesday. Be sure to read chapters eleven and twelve in your textbooks by then. After that it's finals, and then you're all off the hook! See you next time, everybody!"

Enticed by the view outside the open door, most of the students jumped up and hurried out. A few gravitated to the front of the lecture hall with questions for the instructor, and Jan fell in with them.

After two or three minutes, the other students had moved on. "Excuse me, Fred?" she asked.

Fred turned away from his lesson notes. "Oh, hi, Jan. What can I help you with?"

"Oh, I was curious about Wheeler. Is there any more information about him?"

"Not much. At least not yet. Some enterprising soul may find some additional information. But for now, he seems to have dropped off the map completely. Why do you ask? Do you know someone who has one of his prints?"

"Actually …" Jan took an extra breath. "… I may be related to him."

Fred did a quick double-take. "Well, then, I should be asking you for more information, shouldn't I?"

"No, I don't know any more than you do." Jan shrugged. "Well, not much. I know that my mom's maiden name is Wheeler, and she—and my grandma, when she was still with us—used to say that my grandfather was a professional photographer." She gave a half-smile. "They also said quite a few other things about him that were less charitable."

"Did he skip town on them?"

"No, I don't think so. Grandma said she caught him sleeping around and divorced him. She said he was a deadbeat, a cheapskate, and obviously a philanderer. Those are the printable terms."

"And the family has no contact with him?"

"I don't think they want any."

"Hmmm." Fred absentmindedly scratched one of his cheeks. "It might be interesting to see if he's the same guy, and if he knows what's going on with his old photographs. Think you could find out?"

"Well, I could try."

"If you get a lead on this guy, let me know. I'd be interested in seeing whether he really is the slimeball your grandma makes him out to be. And in any case, I'd like to see how he responds to the recent news."

TWO

It was always a little disorderly in the apartment, but there was nothing Jan's mother could do about it. She kept three cats, and it was impossible to keep things completely neat with any more than two. Otherwise, the place was tidy, as Jan had always remembered her house to be in her childhood.

Now her mother sat in an easy chair, brows knitted and lips pursed, while Jan perched on the adjoining cloth sofa and brushed absentmindedly at a few remaining cat hairs that had strayed onto the upholstery.

"Why in hell would you want to contact *him*, Janice?"

Jan related the conversation she'd had with Fred Lopez. "Why wouldn't it be worth finding out?"

"Janice, you stay away from that man. I'm warning you, he's nothing but trouble."

"He's your father, isn't he?"

Jan's mother rose a few inches out of her chair, her face suddenly red. Slowly, as she brought herself under control, she settled back down again.

"I'm going to assume," she said at length, "that you were simply wondering why I wouldn't want any further contact with my father, not flipping shit at me."

"I'm sorry, Mom," Jan said. "I didn't mean to cause offense. I just thought you might wonder about him sometimes."

"'S all right." Jan's mother took a deep breath. "He's never really acted like a father, so I don't think of him as one.

"I remember him being around the house when I was a very little girl. It was a pretty typical household then. Dad went to work, Mom stayed home. But I don't remember much of that. I was five years old when they got divorced, and then it was just me and Mom. I saw Dad every few weeks or so for a while after that, but he wasn't really involved any more.

"And then the accident happened."

Jan responded by rote. "The one when you were six years old. Your leg got cut open on a playground and you almost died."

"Uh-huh. Nobody knew how the slide had been damaged, but it was sharp as a butcher knife." That sentence always turned up in the story, and Jan had grown up hearing how that slide was as sharp as a butcher knife. "Fortunately for me," her mother concluded, "someone saw me get hurt and called an ambulance right away. But by the time I got there, I'd lost so much blood that I could have died.

"The hospital was able to find me a donor in time—just barely. But do you think they could have asked your grandfather? Not likely! He wasn't even there. His daughter was dying, and he couldn't be bothered to lift a fucking finger."

"He still lived in town, then?" Jan asked.

"Yeah. The divorce didn't leave him with enough money to support his loose old ways, but he still ran a portrait studio and did work for department stores. Then, one day, he left."

"Did he stop paying alimony or child support—skip town? Or did he just move away?"

"Beside the payments—and he was legally required to make those—he broke off all other contact with the family. I never saw him again after the accident." The older woman's face showed her anger and pain. "According to Mom, he paid his alimony and child support, but that was all. He did nothing else. And as soon as I got married, the child support stopped.

"About the time he left, Mom had to get a job. It was a hard time for women trying to enter the workplace, because so many of the jobs were going back to the men after the war. Times were hard for us. But once again, he couldn't be bothered to help."

Jan thought for a minute. It seemed as though something was missing, but she couldn't quite place it. Finally, she asked, "What do you think his problem was?"

Her mother gave a bitter little smile. "I think he suffered from a mental and psychological defect."

"What kind of a defect?"

"A penis," her mother said.

Jan raised her eyebrows; her mother continued. "Well, it does seem to work that way, doesn't it, Jan? Do you remember anything about your own father? Where is he? Where is the support he promised?"

Jan had no answer. She had only the vaguest memories of her father, only a ghostly image of a grinning, lanky, brown-haired man. He had left when she was two years old, and she hadn't seen him since she was five.

"But you and I got by, didn't we?" her mother asked. "Not easy, but we made it work—the same way that your grandmother and I made things work.

"It's up to you whether you want to find Wheeler or not." Jan's mother had a wary expression as she continued. "I don't know where he is or how to find him. I think I still have the address and phone number of Mom's old divorce lawyer. If his firm is still in business, they might have a forwarding address in their records. But I'm telling you, *be careful.*"

Of course, the divorce lawyer had long since retired and more recently died. But fortunately for Jan, he had raised and trained a daughter and a son to continue his practice.

Jan had recognized his name immediately, because his children had left it prominently attached to the firm. Everyone who lived in the Bay Area and owned a television set had heard of Mick Callahan and Associates, LLC; they specialized in personal-injury and divorce cases, chased ambulances, and produced their own commercials. Their mewling advertising jingle, written and performed by a friend of the Callahan family who owned a guitar, was embedded beyond extraction in Jan's head as she opened the office door.

"Can I help you?"

Hubby acting like a prick? Better call Mick!

"Yes, thanks. I'm Janice Gibson. Clara Wheeler Gibson is my mom, and Dora MacKinnon Wheeler was my grandmother. I'm looking for a forwarding address."

Quack doctor makin' you sick? Better call Mick!

"Hmmm … Wheeler … Wheeler … Um, did this have to do with your mom's divorce, or your grandma's?"

When your family rights are on the line,

"My grandmother's, thank you."

Or injuries keep you from feelin' fine,

"Let me take down your information, and we'll look up the file. We'll need to set up an appointment to answer your question after the search is complete, and that will be billed as standard time."

We'll get you justice, jiffy quick!

"Okay, thanks."

Better call Mick!

Better call Mick!

Better call Mick!

About three days later, Jan had returned to the office and sat across an ancient, weathered mahogany desk—Mick's own, possibly—from an expensively-dressed woman with a permanent and persistent sinus condition.

"Maeve Callahan. Pleased to meet you," the woman said with a snuffle.

"Janice Gibson, likewise," Jan responded.

"Yes. Well—*snrk*—" Callahan said, "this was an interesting case, wasn't it? Fellow caught red-handed with some chick named Zoë, unable to keep it in his pants. But we watched him like a hawk after we won the case, and we made sure he made his payments on time. Because *that's what we do*."

"Do you have a current forwarding address for him?"

"*Snnrrrrrrrrkk!*"

"Um, gesundheit."

"Oh, never mind that. It's the damn fog. Blocks me up like a goddamned caved-in mine. Anyway, we've got an address, but it's just the forwarding address the respondent left us after the petitioner died. Don't know if it's current; never had to use it. *Snrk*."

"Okay, what is it?"

Callahan handed Jan a business card. On the back was the number of a post office box in Casper, Wyoming.

"You might try contacting the post office and see if the respondent still owns that box, and if not, whether he left a forwarding address. But as I say—*snrk*—we never had occasion to contact him after the alimony terms ended, so I can't tell you from there."

Jan stood up to leave. "Well, thank you for the help," she said, while privately musing over how little actual work her three hundred dollars represented.

"No problem at all. And remember—*snrk*—if you ever find yourself in domestic trouble or any sort of injury …"

"'Better call Mick.' I'll keep that in mind, thanks."

THREE

On the way through southern Wyoming on Interstate 80, there is a long stretch punctuated only by places named after rocks. Rock Springs, Point of Rocks, Table Rock, Red Desert. In each of these places people had once settled, but from most of them they have since moved on. Only the rocks remain, along with some low grasses and sage. The Interstate ascends ridges and traverses broad basins through some of the most desolate scenery in the United States.

In the many hours required to reach Rawlins and start driving northward, in the absence of the occasional caribou herd or some similar point of focus, a large section of the driver's mind lies fallow. Janice Gibson spent the time and unused capacity walking absentmindedly back through the telephone conversation she'd had with the postmaster at the Casper main post office.

"No, I'm sorry, Janet …"

"Janice, thanks."

"We don't have that name in any of our current records." From the sound of her voice, the postmaster was somewhere in her forties or fifties. She spoke with a slight regional drawl. "It looks like the current holder of that post box is a guy out west of town who makes survival gear."

"I don't know when the man I'm looking for would have had the post box. It might have been years and years ago."

"Well, in that case, it would be tough to track him down. We keep a forwarding address for one year after an address change. But after that, it's a pain to track down the information again ... Wait a minute. What?"

"What?" Jan echoed back.

"We've got an old guy here who's been with us for a long time. Hang on."

Jan did so. Eventually the postmaster picked back up. "Tom's telling me he remembers a guy who used to come into town once a month or so, and he usually had some big parcels to pick up. Your guy wasn't a photographer, was he?"

"He was, actually."

"Well, according to Tom, a lot of the packages came from Kodak. Probably supplies."

"Does Tom have any idea where he went?"

Another long pause. "Not really. He says he thinks the guy went north. Lander, Riverton, Shoshoni. Maybe Thermop."

"Thermop?"

"Oh, sorry. Thermopolis. It's a bit further north, but not as far as Yellowstone. Little town with a big hot spring in it."

"Oh, okay." Jan was writing furiously. "Thanks for your help."

After she turned north at Rawlins and headed toward the towns that the postmaster had suggested, Jan noticed that conditions got a bit less severe—still rugged, rocky and dry, but in the river bottoms there were irrigated fields and small but living towns, green with cottonwoods and the occasional defiant lawn.

In each of the little towns, as she worked her way northward, the first thing she did was to find one of the little kiosks that indicated a public phone. (To her surprise, the rate of technological change in some of the towns was so slow that she could still find full-sized booths, often provisioned with up-to-date phone books.) She tried scanning the phone book for J. Wheelers and ended up calling one or two. But they missed matching the description on some significant point; one of them, a Julia Wheeler, treated Jan to a half-hour tirade about how her little box camera must have been engineered by Satan himself and how her family snapshots never came out the way they should.

Meanwhile, the habit most people had of simply tearing off the pages they needed made Jan's search more difficult. She spent a significant amount of time mulling over how there must be a better way of providing people with the information in the books. She was pretty sure that some of the technologists back in Silicon Valley must be thinking about it.

Jan averaged a couple of towns a day, stopping in little motels as she went. In the towns where she spent the night, she could peruse the motel's phone book and business directory, and she got better information. But it still led her nowhere specific. By the time she turned off the light in her room in Shoshoni and attempted to knead the mattress into a tolerable level of suppleness, she was pretty miserable. All of her research had led her nowhere at all. She was also getting pretty damned sick of the smell of Lysol.

In the morning, Jan handed the directories back to the owner of the motel. "Thanks for letting me look over these last night. I didn't find what I was looking for, but I appreciate the help."

"No problem, hon." The woman behind the counter pushed up her almond-shaped glasses absentmindedly. "I don't want to pry, but what *are* you looking for?"

"I understand that my grandfather is living in this area somewhere. There was a bad divorce, and I've never really met him."

"Then why look for the jackass now?"

Jan hesitated. "I think," she said, "that I should probably go over that with him first. If I can find him."

"Oh, okay, hon. Like I said, I'm sorry if I'm prying."

"It's no problem."

"Do you know anything about him?"

"Only his name and his profession. Or at least what his profession used to be. He's a photographer named J.W. Wheeler."

The woman behind the counter looked up abruptly. "I've heard of him," she said. "I think my friend April had a nephew who had him do his senior portraits. They looked pretty darn good, if I remember right. Let me see if I can get hold of April for you."

Half an hour later, the motel owner hung her phone up at last. "Well, hell. April doesn't have any information, and neither does her brother. They say that Josiah—that's the nephew—set the whole thing up himself. So they don't know how to get hold of Wheeler."

"Could I talk to Josiah directly?"

"Naw, he's overseas with the Army. Germany, I think. He's not married yet, and I don't think he's got a girlfriend waiting for him here, so I'm pretty much panned out. I'm awfully sorry." The woman thought for a moment. "I'm not sure I'm remembering this right or just imagining it, but I think April said once that Josiah'd had to go up to Thermop to have his pictures taken."

"Well, that's my next stop," Jan said.

"Next stop, Thermop," said the motel owner with a grin. "Well, if he's around there, he shouldn't be too difficult to find. You may have noticed these towns out here are a bit smaller than out in San Fran."

"Yeah, I guess so."

Once Jan had worked up sufficient tact to extricate herself from her hostess's small talk and get back to the northward road, she tried simultaneously to enjoy her freshly restored spirits and to calm herself. If Wheeler was really still in Thermopolis, what was about to happen? Would he welcome her or throw her out? Had he actually been the villain her mother had described to her? If so, would he still be defiant, or bitter, or penitent? What if he was an unctuous creep? Or violent?

Jan didn't even know what he looked like. She could walk right past him in the middle of Thermopolis and neither one of them would ever know it.

Meawhile, the road wound its way around a huge artificial reservoir and into the mouth of a deep canyon. The surroundings were still redolent with naked rocks, and stripes of dun, white, and reddish brown on the canyon walls marked the way forward. Jan drove into the canyon.

And drove.

And *drove.*

Just when it seemed that the canyon would stretch on forever, Jan emerged into the open again. The road wound its way through a few additional irrigated fields, and then she was there.

It was much like the chain of towns she'd been exploring over the previous few days—old frame houses, newer ramblers and ranch houses, pavement cracked with the harsh summers and winters, small roadside businesses.

And then, just past the high school, Jan was suddenly out of town. Reacting quickly, she ducked into a small turnaround loop. But she quickly brought the car to a stop as she realized that this wasn't just a turnaround.

In front of her, past the end of the loop and a set of railroad tracks, flowed the same Bighorn River that the road had followed since she left Shoshoni that morning. Beyond that, the far bank of the river was coated in a thick, globular coating of white tinged with stripes of yellow, red, and brown.

It looked like a sheet cake frosted by a baker on LSD.

Around the giant psychedelic cake were bathhouses, water slides, and a tall, conical hill completely devoid of life of any sort—not even the deep green bushes and sage that dotted the other hills around town. Human beings had been there at some point and added giant letters in crushed white rock:

WORLDS LARGEST
MINERAL
HOT SPRING

A chain of giant arrows, made of the same crushed white rock, pointed downward and to the right, toward the area where most of the bathhouses were. Over the river hung a suspension footbridge which seemed to lead nowhere specific on its nearer side. Jan began to detect a heavy tinge of sulfur in the air.

"Well," she said to herself, "it's certainly different."

Jan pulled the car back into town and looked for public telephones along the main drag. She found one a few blocks from the hot springs, but the phone book was missing. At another one, the phone book was still there, but completely mutilated. She changed tactics and went looking for a business that might have some information.

She noticed a small shop with a sandwich board standing by the curb:

GIFTS - SOUVENIRS - CURIOS
NAILS by KATE
(By Appointment—Please Call)

Jan stopped the car in front of the shop, walked to the door, and stepped inside.

From somewhere in the building, a recording of big band jazz was playing. But in among all of the counters and tables stacked with wood plaques, carved onyx statuettes, and T-shirts, it was impossible to pinpoint the location of the loudspeakers. In a darkened back corner stood a nail-finishing table and an ancient hair dryer, of the sort under which postwar women used to sit in heavy curlers.

Jan heard a shuffling sound, followed by brisk, clicking steps. In a few seconds, a smallish woman stepped in. Her steel-gray hair was drawn back and bound in a clasp adorned with a small concho. The simple, almost utilitarian blue blouse and tan slacks she wore accented her trim, well-kept figure. Her dark eyes, lively and inquisitive, locked in on Jan.

"Good afternoon," she said. "How can I help you?"

Jan answered, "I'm looking for a photographer named J.W. Wheeler. Do you know where I might find him?"

"Oh, sure," the woman said. She pulled a tourist map from a stack of them on the counter in front of her and began to draw on it. "He's three blocks down ..." she drew an arrow back along the highway by which Jan had entered town, "... and four blocks west." In a precise script, she wrote down an address. "You can't miss it. Or if you do, you'll be out of town, and you'll turn around and come back. You can't really get lost in a town this size."

"Thanks. Are you Kate?"

"That's me," the woman grinned. "But you're not local, are you?"

"No, just passing through."

"So why are you looking for Jim? You didn't come all this way just to have a portrait taken. I don't think his reputation extends that far out."

"Well, you might be surprised," Jan said. "Anyway, I need to talk to him. I'm Janice Gibson, by the way."

Kate stiffened, and it seemed to Jan that the older woman's hair followed suit.

"God damn it!" Kate said. "God damn it to hell!"

"What? What did I say?"

"I just told you where he was. If I'd known who you were, I wouldn't have given you a word."

"Excuse me?"

Kate leaned across the counter and glared intently into Jan's eyes. "You leave him alone," she said. "He's of no use to you. He doesn't have much money. He's an old man now. Leave him in peace."

Jan was balancing unevenly between disorientation and anger, as though she had just been punched without warning. "Look," she said unsteadily, "I don't know what you're talking about. I'm not here to swindle him, but I do have a message for him. Thank you for the address."

She turned and left the shop without allowing Kate a chance to respond.

It took the better part of an hour before Jan was composed enough to consider going to the address Kate had given her. Finally, she parked her car in front of a trim old house with an enclosed porch. Instead of a back yard, the house appeared to lead to a small greenhouse finished in frosted glass, which was the most incongruous thing Jan had yet seen here aside from the springs. The front yard was covered in crushed red rock and ornamental pieces of milky quartz, surrounding a trim wooden sign:

J. W. WHEELER
Photographer
Portraits - Agricultural - Industrial

Jan took a couple of final deep breaths, stepped onto the porch, and rang the doorbell.

A minute or two later, the door opened to reveal a man slightly taller than Jan herself. His angular face, adorned with bushy eyebrows and mustache to match his sandy gray hair, seemed reserved and cautious.

"Can I help you?" he asked.

"Mr. Wheeler?"

"That's me," he said with a half-smile. "They say two of me would be one too many."

"My name is Janice Gibson."

Wheeler looked around his feet for a moment, then refocused on Jan. "Clara's little girl?"

Jan smiled. "Yes."

He took a deep breath. "Please come in," he said.

The front door opened into a combination office and showroom. Shades over the windows and the presence of the enclosed porch subdued the hard sunlight outdoors, and track lighting filled out the resulting shadows. Samples of Wheeler's work, covering all of the categories mentioned on the sign outdoors, hung on the walls.

A large mahogany desk stood at the inside end of the room, with two comfortable chairs drawn up in front of it and one leather-upholstered office chair behind. On the back wall, overlooking the room, was a mammoth, razor-sharp, incredibly detailed black-and-white print of Devil's Tower, surmounted with cottony white clouds in an inky black sky.

Wheeler sat down in the office chair and motioned Jan into one of the others. "So what are you doing out here? I'm afraid I'm pretty much tapped out financially, so it can't be that ..."

Something in Jan's mind snapped. After three days of searching and the earlier interlude with Kate, her patience had finally run out.

"Why the *fuck* does everyone think this is about money?" she shouted. "First Mom, then Kate—whoever she is—and now you. *What the fuck is wrong with you people?*"

Wheeler said nothing. Seconds dragged like minutes, and he simply sat with his elbows on the desk and his chin on his folded hands, while his eyes scanned the distance as though searching for phantoms. Finally he straightened, separated his hands, and pointed at Jan.

"First of all," he said, "*language*."

Jan glared back.

"Secondly, I apologize for my presumption. If you heard the same comment from someone else, I regret that. Someone your age wouldn't—or shouldn't—have any concept of how ugly divorces can get, but ours was pretty bad. And after a while, that's all you talk about."

"I've heard a bit," Jan said, cooling down slowly. "That honestly wasn't what brought me out here, though. So we really are ... related?"

Wheeler laughed softly, his eyes still sad. "That's one way of putting it. But you'd be forgiven, I think, for wanting to take it one step at a time. They say that it takes more than biology to make a man a father, so this could be a very touchy situation. But yeah, we're ... related." Another small laugh. "You can start out calling me Jim, if you prefer."

"That might be best, to begin with," Jan said. "It's a lot."

"It is," Wheeler agreed. "So you're still living in The City?"

"San Francisco, yeah."

"You in college?"

"Yeah. I just finished freshman year."

"Nice. What major?"

"I haven't really settled on one."

Wheeler raised one bushy eyebrow. "Clock's ticking."

"I know, I know. It's going to be something art-related, but I haven't really locked anything in yet." Jan paused and took a breath in an attempt to slow the pace of the conversation. "I think I'm leaning toward graphic design."

"Nice," Wheeler said. "You'll find a lot of competition in that field in San Francisco, I think. But that's kind of the way the art business works." He gave her a sidelong glance. "Given any thought to photography?"

Jan laughed. "A little. I've taken a couple of courses."

"What does your mom think?"

Jan pursed her lips. "She thinks graphic design is a great field."

"I'm sure she does."

"So anyway," Jan continued, sidestepping quickly, "one of my college courses is why I'm here. I had to take Art History 101 and 102 if I wanted to pursue any art degree, so I started there. And a couple of weeks before the end of Art History 102, my instructor starts talking about the big photography boom that happened in The City between the twenties and the forties."

"Ah, yes, The Classic Years." Wheeler drew an imaginary marquee in the air with one hand.

"I think it's a specific interest of his. Fred—Fred Lopez is his name—seems to get cranked up when he starts talking about it. Anyway, in the last class before finals week, he was talking to us about the auction price record that they set in 1979."

Wheeler laughed more easily now. "*Moonrise, Hernandez, New Mexico, 1941*," he said. "Twenty-two grand! What a con!" Looking at the surprise on Jan's face, he throttled back. "Sorry, kid. It's just that Adams himself would never have charged that much for a new print back in the old days. I can't imagine what he thought about that!" He continued to chuckle for a few seconds.

"Well, that's not all," Jan said.

"Okay?"

"One of the things Fred told us was that the booming market in photographic art had caused collectors to take an interest ... in you."

Wheeler stopped laughing; he took another long pause.

"Bullshit," he said at last.

Jan pointed at him. "Language."

Wheeler shrugged. "Okay, fair's fair."

"The last thing that Fred showed us was a print that he told us was one of yours. It was an arrangement of old farm tools."

"Farm tools? ... God knows, I've photographed a lot of farm tools since I moved out here, but not ... Oh, wait! There was that barnyard outside of Modesto ..."

"Yeah, that was the one."

"Hang on a second." Wheeler rose and walked quickly into an adjoining room. Jan heard large metal cabinets opening and closing, and drawers being shifted back and forth.

After a few minutes, Wheeler came back with a large black binder. In it, Jan could see the edges of a stack of onionskin sleeves. Wheeler leafed through these for a moment, then carefully pinched the edge of a sheet of paper and drew it out. He opened the binder flat and lay the paper across it.

"This it?" he asked.

The composition was certainly the same, but the image looked different. It seemed deeper somehow, as though Jan might actually reach into it if she wanted. The textures and carved initials on the worn wooden implements seemed almost tangible.

"That's it," Jan said. "But this looks ... a lot more *real*."

"Thanks," Wheeler said. "I did this originally when I was trying to learn about the Zone System. Have they taught you about that?"

"Not yet, not in detail."

"It's a model for shaping a black-and-white negative and the prints you make off of it. Adams was in on it at the beginning, and he gave it most of its publicity. You don't need to use it if you don't want to. But it does give you a lot of detail and texture."

"I guess so. The copy Fred had up didn't look like this one, though, I'll say that."

"On a classroom projector?" Wheeler said. "I'd imagine not. It's a copy of a copy at least, and projection thins the image out."

He carefully put the print back into the binder, using his fingers like tweezers to handle its edges. Then he excused himself for a moment. Jan heard the cabinets and drawers again, and after a moment, Wheeler came back.

"I'll talk to Kate," he said. "Again, things were unpleasant for a few years there. She's a close friend of mine here, so she was in earshot of some of it." He paused. "As far as I know, I never missed a payment. I sent money for birthdays and Christmas, too, but I don't know if your mom ever saw any of it. And you ... this is the first time I've actually met you. I did see a couple of pictures when you were a baby."

"Mom's never mentioned getting anything from you."

"Well, I can document the payments, if there's ever a need for it. But you shouldn't have gotten dragged into that old mess."

The conversation began to slow. "Is this just your business, or is part of it living space, too?" Jan asked.

"It's an all-in one," Wheeler answered. "I talk to customers here, and there's a little portrait room behind the office." He motioned back toward the room where he'd retrieved the binder. "Darkroom's in the basement, and there's a little living space upstairs. It's a nice setup for one old guy."

"What about the greenhouse?"

"Ah, you noticed that, huh? Well, when I first moved up here, I bought the house from a fellow who had owned a flower shop downtown. He did his growing behind the house, most of it."

"Just never got around to taking the greenhouse out?"

Wheeler gave a start. "Why would I take the greenhouse out?"

"Do you grow anything in it?"

"Well, no."

"So why keep it?"

Wheeler sat back and studied Jan intently. "You say you're an art student?"

Jan hesitated, confused. "Yeah."

Wheeler continued scrutinizing her. "You know what?" he said. "I don't think I'm gonna tell you. If you come up with something, you tell me."

"What?"

"Like I said, I'll leave it on the table for a while."

"Okay," said Jan, still feeling off balance. "Can I ask something else?"

"Sure."

"Why did you move?"

Wheeler shrugged. "Money again. San Francisco is an expensive place to live. You may have noticed."

"Uh-huh. But why here?"

"I don't understand."

"With all due respect, this is kind of out in the middle of nowhere. Why would you have wanted to move to a place like this?"

Wheeler was studying Jan again. "You know," he said, "I don't think I'll tell you that either."

"I'm really not getting it."

"I know." Wheeler gave a sly grin. "'What is jazz?'"

Jan slowed down and spoke in measured rhythms. "Okay, look," she said. "You're a creative photographer. Or you used to be. Doesn't it hurt to be all the way out here?"

Wheeler's grin spread a little. "Well, there are the springs," he said.

"And?"

"Exactly." Wheeler straightened his face and pivoted. "Can you stay for dinner?"

"Oh, sorry, no, I can't," Jan said. "I've got to head back. This little fact-finding mission took longer than I expected, so I'll have to get on the road." This answer, while true, was not complete; Jan was acutely aware that she needed to leave before her annoyance started to show. "Thank you for taking the time to talk to me."

"Hey, no problem." Wheeler shrugged again. "Thanks for bringing me the news. You can tell Mr. Martinez ..."

"Lopez. Fred Lopez."

"Right, sorry, tell Mr. Lopez that I'm still kicking. And this is an interesting piece of news. Safe travels, kid."

After he showed Jan back to her car, Wheeler sat at his desk for several minutes, hands folded in front of his face. At length he picked up the receiver of the telephone on the desk and dialed a number, whipping his index finger around in impatient circles.

"Hello?" he said into the phone. "I'm trying to reach Martin Zahn. Yeah, that's right. Thanks." About two minutes later he spoke again. "Martin? Hi, Jim Wheeler up in Thermopolis. Fine, thanks. Kate's good too. I'll tell her you asked. How're Sue and the kids? Good, good.

"Hey, listen. I've just been informed that some of my old work from the thirties and forties has been 'discovered.' Have you heard anything like that? ... Well, could you check into it for me? ... Thanks, man. I appreciate it. Talk to you soon. Yeah, bye."

FOUR

Jan was relieved to get back home, where her hair lay flat and her skin didn't threaten to crumble to powder. In the first week of fall semester, she dug back into the familiar cycle of classes and homework.

On Thursday she walked into the first class of Art History 201, Fred Lopez, instructor. He continued where he'd left off as though there hadn't been a break in his narrative at all, pacing the floor in front of the seats while gesturing at projected slides and running a hand absentmindedly through his shock of thick, dark hair.

At the end of class, the students filed out; only Jan remained behind. "Hi, Fred," she said.

"Hi, Jan," Fred responded. "How was your summer?"

"Very interesting ... very interesting indeed."

"How so?"

"Well," Jan said, with a hint of drama, "remember that lecture where you told us about J.W. Wheeler?"

"Oh, yeah. You said you thought you and he might be related?"

"Yeah. Well, I went looking for my grandfather ... and I found J.W. Wheeler."

"Still alive?"

"Very much so."

"So tell me," Fred asked, "had he heard about his success in the art market?"

"No." Jan laughed. "It came as quite a surprise."

"I imagine so. So is he still local?"

"Not even close. Thermopolis, Wyoming."

Fred paused. "Wow! My mom and dad and I stopped there once on our way back from Yellowstone. Fun place."

"Try 'ass end of the universe,'" Jan said with a smirk.

"That hardly seems fair," Fred cautioned her. "Kind of dismissive, too."

"I call 'em as I see 'em."

"That's a hell of a thing for a student in this program to say."

"You're beginning to sound like Jim."

"I'm encouraged. Say, do you have a picture of him?"

"No," Jan admitted, "I didn't have my camera with me."

Fred scowled and pursed his lips. "You didn't take your camera?"

"No. Shoot me."

"Bang." Fred paused. "So did it seem like he was still doing any creative work?"

"Not really. Mostly family pictures and school portraits, with a few industrial things thrown in."

"Still being a Lothario?"

"Not at all. Just an old guy who lives alone, over his studio. He was never impolite to me in any way, and all of the locals send their kids over to have their school portraits done."

Jan spent a few minutes telling Fred about her adventures and what she'd seen at Wheeler's house.

"So at the end of all of this, he gets all weird and starts not answering my questions," she continued. "I asked how he'd ended up living there, and I asked him about his house, and he just starts saying, 'I don't think I'm going to tell you … hee, hee, hee!' I think he might be going senile!"

"Don't be so sure. So he's living in Thermopolis?"

"That's what I said."

"And he bought a house with a big frosted greenhouse in the back yard, which he refuses to tear down?"

"Yeah, we went over this."

Fred smiled, much the way that Wheeler had smiled. "I think he's still creating. I don't know what he's doing with his prints, or if he's just stockpiling negatives. But he's doing something—possibly a lot of something."

"Out there in the middle of nowhere?"

"Well," Fred said, grinning, "there are the springs."

"Oh, for God's sake. What are you getting at?"

Fred started to laugh. "I don't think I'm going to tell you either."

The pitch and volume of Jan's voice were beginning to get out of her control. "Don't you sit there and play the same stupid-ass games with me!"

"All right," Fred answered her. "Got half an hour for a visit to the library?"

"Yeah," she said. "My next class is at three."

"Good. Let me lock up here and we'll go."

At the University Library, Fred led Jan past most of the bookshelves and down a carpeted hallway. He turned aside into the Cartography Room, where shelves of atlases and drawers of detailed maps stood in close company. Fred rummaged around for a few minutes and finally spread out an oversized atlas on a counter. He motioned Jan over to look at the page he'd selected.

"Okay, here's Thermopolis, right here. See it?" he asked.

"Yeah, I know where it is. I had lots of maps when I went," Jan said.

"Okay, fine. And here's Yellowstone. It's a day's drive away."

"All right."

"And right next to it, to the south, there are the Tetons and Jackson Hole."

"All right."

"Over this way ..." Fred traced a line upward and to the right, northeastward, with his finger, "... is Bear Lodge. What Anglos call Devil's Tower."

"Oh, yeah," Jan said. "He had a picture of it in his office. I'd forgotten."

"Okay. A day's drive *this* way," Fred traced southward, "is Rocky Mountain National Park."

"I hadn't thought about that."

"Well, it's in Colorado, but it's not that far away from him. Also down in southern Wyoming, parts of the Oregon Trail are worn so deep that there are permanent grooves in the rock. A guy like Wheeler could make something out of that." Fred looked at Jan. "So what do all of these things have in common?"

"Beats me."

"A bunch of the big photographic artists of the Group *f*/64 generation—Adams and Weston, some of the others—didn't spend much time working outside California. Oh, Adams has *Moonrise* and a handful of other things, but a lot of his stuff and much of Weston's, and many of the others' as well, was centered in California. They couldn't really do otherwise, because so much of California was new to the white population. It was all they had time for."

"So you're saying that Jim settled himself in the middle of as much new material as he could find."

"Exactly. Thermopolis isn't the middle of nowhere, it's the middle of everywhere. And that doesn't even touch on smaller things closer to him that only locals really know about. Between all of that and his greenhouse, he could have amassed a huge backlog of work by now."

"So what's the deal with the greenhouse, anyway?" Jan asked. "This obviously means something to you, but it didn't to me."

On the wall behind the map cabinets, someone had hung a print of the famous scene, from Georges Méliès's *A Trip to the Moon*, in which the Man in the Moon has had his right eye shot out. Fred looked at it and smiled to himself. "That question," he said, "I think I'll leave to you."

"Bite me," said Jan.

"That's no way to address your teacher," Fred answered.

INTERLUDE: 1938

It wasn't a change in the weather. There never really was a change in the weather in San Francisco, Jim thought, just fluctuations in the texture of the moisture outside. Here, in place of bright leaves and bonfires, the moisture just got coarse enough to fall out of the air and onto the ground.

He could hear the drizzle on the windows outside his small studio office as he shuffled papers around his desk, preparing invoices and entering figures in his ledger. It would have been nice to hire an accountant, but his business wasn't financially mature enough yet. With a bit of luck, tonight's shoot would lead to bigger things.

There was a knock at the door, rapid and precise. It echoed off the wallpaper, woodwork, and hardwood floors in the business. By the time it reached Jim's ears, it had acquired a hollow, tinny sound. The knocking of his steps reverberated back, accompanying him to the door.

A trim-looking young woman stood outside the door. "Hello, I'm Zoë Quinlan," she said in a voice deeper than her height would have suggested. "I'm here for the shoot. May I come in?"

"Oh, yeah, please do. Jim Wheeler. Pleased to meet you."

"People often are." She flashed him a mischievous grin as she pulled the felt cloche off of her bobbed brown hair. After hanging her coat on a nearby hook, she opened her small purse and rummaged for a moment. "Aha! There's one." She extended a business card in one hand. "My card."

Jim laughed. "Caught me off guard! I'll grab you one of mine on our way back out. Anyway, thanks for dealing with the odd time of day."

"Not a problem. My evenings are all yours. Unless it's Friday, of course, or Saturday. Or if I should suddenly acquire a beau."

Jim counted imaginary numbers on his fingers for a moment. "Got it. At least I think I do."

"So what's up this evening?"

"Well," Jim said, "I've managed to land a deal with Capwell's, doing product shots that will eventually go into their holiday newspaper ads. This is the first time I've done work for them, so I want to put my best foot forward. Or hand, in this case. We're doing jewelry tonight."

"You're speaking my language," Zoë said with a chuckle. "Can't go wrong with jewelry."

"Glad you approve. Which reminds me: Can I see your hands for a moment?"

"Oh, sure." Jim took the young woman's fingertips in his own. "Good, good. Actually, let's step over to the light and do this correctly. Hmmm … nice … good cuticles …"

"Do you need to check my teeth?"

"Hey, come on." Jim made an imploring gesture. "First project. Important client. Remember? If they keep hiring me, maybe I can keep hiring you. Nice nails, though. The color's a bit dramatic, isn't it?"

"I tried to pick something that would look good on film."

"Oh, thanks for the thought. Well, the studio is right through here."

Jim had been working under his own shingle for about three years, and although the little studio was modestly appointed, he regarded it with some pride. Inside dark curtains that covered three of the four walls stood four scoops with a variety of scrims and barndoors attached to them. In their midst was a chair, a table under a black velvet drape, and a small view camera with its bellows stretched wide.

He motioned toward the chair. "Sit down, please, and put your hands on the table. Excuse me a moment." There was a rummaging commotion, and he returned from behind one of the curtains. "Okay, please put the ring on your right hand. Will it fit one of the fingers there? Good! And put the watch on your left wrist." Zoë did so. "And hold on for a minute ..."

Jim repositioned two of the lights and adjusted the accessories on two of the others. He ducked under the focusing cloth and twiddled the knobs, then looked out and ducked in again, then finally returned.

He reached toward her hands. "May I?"

"Huh? Oh, sure."

Jim carefully grasped the ring, ducked under the cloth a third time, and slowly turned it from side to side. "Ah, there's the sparkle. All right, don't move!"

Jim flipped the cloth over the backplane of the camera and leaned over for a couple of film holders. He slid a holder into place in the backplane, drew out the darkslide, and said, "Now hold as still as you can." He grabbed a cable release and smoothly squeezed the button with his thumb. "Okay, keep holding still if possible. I'm going to do a few backups." He replaced the slide, withdrew the holder, rechecked the focusing screen, flipped the holder over, and took a second exposure. He then repeated the process with the other film holder, took one final look at the screen, and sat back.

"You can move now," he said, putting the two film holders into a small wooden box marked SHOT in neat hand-lettering.

"Oooofff!" answered Zoë, stretching her arms. "Between the cramping and the heat, it could be a long evening. Those lights are pretty toasty."

"Yeah, sorry about that. Maybe somebody will come up with a better system one of these days, but they haven't cracked it yet." Jim motioned toward the two windows on the wall behind him. "If I had my druthers, I'd just as soon use sunlight for everything, but you can't for this kind of work. You can't really control it precisely enough. It's a shame, too. This part of the country has gorgeous sunlight."

"When you can get it," Zoë observed.

Jim smiled back. "Right. Could be worse, though. They say the light is gorgeous in Seattle. But just try finding some! I need the watch and the ring back, please."

"Oh, right. Just a moment ... here you go."

"Thank you. I'll go and get the next item. We'll do one of the bracelets next." Jim retreated, rummaged, and returned. "Okay, put that on. This'll be a bit easier—just silver, no rocks. Hold on ... now keep your hand still for a moment ... hold it ... hold it ... and done." Two more film holders went into the box. "Bracelet back, please."

As Jim rummaged for the next piece of jewelry, Zoë called out, "How long have you been doing this?"

Jim's returning voice sounded muffled. "What do you mean by 'this?' Photography in general, or this studio?"

"Oh, I don't know. I don't think I'd broken it down that far."

Jim came back with some more rings. "Okay, try these on. Let's go for one on each hand."

"You're giving me a ring for my left hand? Why, this is so sudden!"

"Let's keep moving, please. We've still got quite a few of these to do. And nothing personal, but I'm a married man." He held up his own left hand to show the dull link of metal on his own ring finger.

"Pffft," said Zoë, arranging her hands on the table. "Happily?"

"Mostly."

"Hardly a ringing endorsement, there, fella."

"Sooo … to answer your earlier question … I got my first job assisting a photographer in town about five years ago. I worked for him for a couple of years, then I branched out on my own. That was about three years ago."

Zoë looked around the camera to study his face. "How old are you, anyway?" she asked.

"Twenty-one."

"So you started with this other fellow at sixteen, and went into business for yourself at eighteen?"

"Yep." Jim looked at the table. "We need to get your hands back into position. Overlap a bit higher up, make sure both rings are visible."

"Oh, sorry."

"Don't mention it. Hold, please … keep holding … keep holding … good, thanks."

"Man, those lights are warm," Zoë said. "No offense, but have you got any gravy? I could use a good basting."

"Funny, you didn't look like the masochistic type."

Zoë laughed. “I’m not. Although it might help with the lights.”

Jim collected the two rings, then went behind the curtain for more. “How about you?”

“How about I what?”

“Come from around here?”

“Oh, yeah. I’m a Marin County girl originally.”

“Been modeling long?”

Zoë paused. “Well, not too long. We’re getting close to things a gentleman isn’t supposed to ask a lady.”

“I wasn’t going to pursue the point, don’t worry. But I have a professional interest. Do you do fashion modeling, or similar work?”

“Not much yet. I’m hoping to get to that point, though.”

“Well, we have a common interest in making sure this shoot comes off well, then.”

“So, where do *you* want to take *this* business?” Zoë asked.

Jim came back to the table. “Here, try these on. I’d be happy if it just kept the lights on and food on the table. I’d be happier still if it gave me the opportunity to do some extracurricular work.”

“Oooh, an *artiste!*”

“Left hand a little upward, please. Hang on … may I?”

“Sure.”

Jim adjusted a bracelet to catch the light for the camera. “Hold there … hold … hold … done, thanks.” He took the latest batch of jewelry back.

"I know a guy at the *Tribune,*" Jim continued as he went for another batch. "His name's Jerry Dumont. He helped me land this job, actually. Anyway, Jerry edits public announcements for the *Trib*. Not glamorous. But he keeps saying he has a novel he wants to finish. He says that any writer you meet, no matter what they write, secretly wants to be a novelist or a poet. I guess it's the same principle with photographers.

"When I got that first apprenticeship, it got me into town. And once I was here, I could go look at people's shows and pick up ideas." Jim grinned. "That kind of thing is dangerous. It makes you wonder how you might stack up once you'd learned enough technique. Here you go."

"Thanks."

Eventually, they had worked through all of the jewelry samples. Zoë stood up, stretched luxuriantly, and rubbed her wrists.

"Oh, man," she exclaimed. "I'm going right home and straight into a long, hot bath. I feel like my arms are in knots."

"Thanks again for your patience tonight," Jim told her. "And now, if you would be so kind, please step through there and wait in the office for a moment."

"Okay, why?"

"I need to do a quick inventory before you can leave."

"You're kidding, right? I mean, it's pretty stuff, but it ain't Tiffany's."

"Just paperwork, my dear. I'll make it quick."

Zoë sat at the desk and looked at the clutter scattered across it. She made note of the framed portrait sitting at the corner of the desktop: an attractive blonde wearing tight curls and a vaguely disinterested expression.

Jim stepped in. "Everything's checked in, accounted for, and locked up, so we can both go home now." He noted the time on a pad of paper, opened the drawer, and pulled out one of his business cards, which he handed to Zoë. "Here you go, before I forget again."

"Thanks." Zoë motioned at the portrait. "Your wife, I presume?"

"Yep, that's Dora."

"Pretty."

"Thanks." Jim helped Zoë into her coat. "I'll develop and contact-print the negatives first thing tomorrow morning. I think we did pretty well, but if we need any retakes, I'll call you then. And if they like the photos at Capwell's and send me more work, I'll be calling you when they do."

"Glad to hear it," Zoë said as Jim opened the front door for her. "Good meeting you, Jim. Talk to you soon."

"Talk to you soon, Zoë."

After Zoë stepped down to the sidewalk, Jim stood in the doorway for a minute or two and watched her swivel and click her way down the street. He smiled, shook his head, and went back inside to shut the studio down for the night.

Jim reported home about half an hour later. Dora was sitting in the living room, reading.

"Evening, dear," Jim called out as he entered.

"You're late tonight," said Dora without looking up.

"I had a jewelry shoot for Capwell's," Jim explained. "I had a hand model come in after work—she had another booking, so I had to wait a bit."

"A hand model?"

"Yep. She puts on the rings and bracelets, and I photograph her hands."

"It doesn't sound like something you should be paying for. Why couldn't *I* put on the jewelry, and you photograph *my* hands?"

"Well," Jim explained, "a hand model has to take special care of her hands. Or his; there's men's jewelry too, of course. Hand models have to be careful not to build up too many calluses, they can't have noticeable scars, they have to keep their skin looking healthy and their cuticles trimmed, and so on.

Jim glanced at Dora. "It goes without saying that they don't chew their nails," he said.

His wife abruptly dropped her right hand from her teeth to her waist. "Oh, so you're paying some young cookie to neglect her housework," she said with a derisive snort.

Jim rolled his eyes. "Good night, Dora," he said, walking toward the hallway that led to the bedroom.

FIVE

Janice guided her car eastward along the interstate, through the same stony near-desert expanses she had traversed the previous year. As she inched ahead through the hours of emptiness, she thought back over the past several months.

She was now finished with the required art history overview courses, so her contact with Fred Lopez was likely to be less frequent in the future. But she was left with a nagging suspicion that the art history coursework in her sophomore year had ended up being more concerned with photographic art than either she or Fred had expected.

First, of course, Fred had announced the confirmation of Wheeler's continued existence to the class. He had given Jan high praise for her detective work, calling on her to stand up so that he could point her out to her fellow students, a gesture she hated. She had stood up quickly, given a painful combination of a smile and a grimace, and immediately sat down again.

Second, in April, Ansel Adams had died. That had derailed the syllabus for a week while Fred had gone over the man's contributions to the art form in which he had worked.

"It's important to keep in mind," he had told the class, "that Adams was more of a settler than an explorer. Based on the amount of material you see about him in the press lately, you'd be excused for thinking that he was the one pivotal talent and voice in early photographic art. Are there any music majors in the room?" Fred had scanned the large class and pointed to an upraised hand. "Okay, Mary, who invented classical music?"

The dark, attractive woman he had just cornered had shifted uneasily in her seat. "What do you mean by that?" she asked. "Do you mean actual Classical music, or do you mean Western orchestral music in general? And what part of it? The structure of it, instrumentation, theory, forms, all came from different people. So what are you asking for?"

"Very good, Mary, thank you. So if I were to change the question, and ask whether Mozart created classical music, what would you think?"

"That would be phrasing the question in the wrong way," Mary had responded. "The art wouldn't be the same without him, but he didn't create it from scratch. He extended it in several ways which grabbed people's attention at a time when they were receptive, and he opened new avenues of exploration and development."

"Excellent, excellent!" Fred had been grinning at this point. "And that is the role that Adams played in photography. He didn't make it an art; other people did that, from Fox Talbot in the beginning to Stieglitz and Weston just before Adams himself. But with his technical improvements, he enlarged the space that photographers could work in. And he legitimized his medium, gave it a face that people would recognize. Just like Mozart did, when you think about it.

"Plus, he set an example for social responsibility among artists of his kind. Much of the preserved wild land that we have in California was protected with his help and advocacy. And he once got into some trouble with his fellow photographers for selling portfolios too cheaply, but his attitude was that if students wanted to see his work, they should have access to it—even if he didn't make top dollar on it."

And then, Jan had received the letter from Wheeler. She had immediately taken it directly to Fred.

"You are going to go, aren't you?" he had asked.

"I don't know," Jan had said. "Last summer ended up being a bit weird, so I've got mixed feelings about it."

"Yeah, but being the darkroom assistant to a recognized artist could be an important item on your resume if you ended up as a photography major. Plus, you may still find out more about the remaining mysteries in your family history."

"That's a little bit scary."

"I know, but sometimes it's important to do the scary things. They can be growth opportunities. How long would this be for?"

"Well, I don't think he knows exactly. An art professor at the University of Wyoming—your opposite number there, maybe—has offered him space for an exhibit from August through October. He says he knows what pieces he wants to show, but he needs help printing and getting the finished prints ready. So he'd like me to show up right after the semester ends, mid-June or so. Probably about six weeks."

"Well, give it some thought. And if you go, be sure to take your camera," Fred had told her.

Jan had checked in with her mother about the letter, as well. She'd also told her mother about her meeting with Wheeler, and about the birthday and Christmas gifts. Her mother had responded bluntly.

"Bullshit," she had said. "I never got anything like that. What was he doing with those checks? Sending them down a black hole or something?"

"I don't know, Mom. I'm just relating what he told me, at the moment."

"Well, let me remind you, your grandmother and I never got anything from him other than what the lawyers could get by twisting his arm. If you intend to maintain any kind of contact with him, you be very, very careful. I'm warning you."

After an endless day of creeping to the east like a bug on a plate, Jan took an exit in Laramie and drove to a university campus completely unlike her own. Following the directions in Wheeler's most recent letter, she navigated past Fraternity Row and between isolated, evenly spaced buildings to arrive at last in front of an auditorium building.

Exiting her car, she looked quickly around herself. Over the distant prairie, evening was beginning to fall. The scent of the hardy evergreens that adorned the campus, along with the ever-present perfume of sage, spiced the clean, dry air. She took a couple of deep, cleansing breaths, then locked her car and stepped into the auditorium.

The scene was just like one of Fred's classes: rows of students sloped as though in a theatre, a desk and a screen at the front of the large space, images projected on a screen behind the desk, and a lecturer gesturing at the images. But the lecturer here was Wheeler.

He seemed more animated now than when Jan had seen him the previous summer, his nods and shrugs having given way to sweeping hand and finger movements. His dress, which included a silver bolo tie and a camel-hair brown Western jacket complete with pearl buttons, bordered on self-parody.

"Basically, I was looking for a defensible middle ground," Wheeler told his audience. "Has anyone here had to study the history of photography in the early part of the century?" Seeing no response, he adjusted tack and continued. "All right. What you need to know is that the earliest photographers who wanted to elevate their work to the level of art figured they'd need to match the standards of the artists, especially painters, who were working at that time.

"So this was in the late 1800s, right? Well, what kind of painters were working back then? Anybody?"

A student spoke up, with some hesitation. "French Impressionists?"

"Exactly!" Wheeler pointed back at him. "And along with the other artists who were working back then, they were shifting away from a literal interpretation of their subject matter. So the first photographic artists joined in right there. Between the methods of that time and the state of the technology they were using—it was still pretty crude—the work they were producing had a vague look to it. They were going for what was called a 'painterly' effect, and at its best, it was.

"But there were a lot of blobs on paper, too. Basically, photographers were trying to mimic the painting of the time and coming up with mostly inferior imitations.

"So around the turn of the century, some younger photographers started to pull away from the imitative approach. They took smaller steps at first, but they were shifting toward making better use of their own medium and the way it behaved. So you had Stieglitz and Steichen, and many of the best pictorialists, who were starting to use the tools based on their own behaviors and strengths. There were still a lot of blobs on paper, though.

"And then, by the twenties, younger photographers were insisting that the blobs had to go. The technical aspects of photography had to be refined as far as they would go, and at that point, the medium would essentially define itself. The images produced would adhere to the highest standards of composition, and they would be sharp, clear, and well-defined. And eventually, this kind of thinking reached its high point when Group *f*/64 formed in the Bay Area in the early thirties. This is when you start hearing the famous names you're familiar with—Edward Weston, Ansel Adams, Imogen Cunningham, and the rest. Some of them were hard-liners of this new school of thought. Others had started out as pictorialists, but they'd never been lazy about it, so they had come to agree with the new approach.

"The old pictorialist images, and the older 'painterly' images, were banished completely. The group's name referred to the tiniest lens opening available on their cameras, which meant that nothing was ever out of focus. They took as their enemy the 'fuzziness' in the older work, and did their own work so that no 'fuzziness' would ever appear.

"And with apologies for the excessive use of drama here ..." Wheeler paused for a moment. "... that is where I came in."

He clicked through several images as he spoke. They all appeared to be older photographs, and they were noticeably similar to the ones that Fred had put on screen during his lectures in San Francisco. "I spent a couple of years apprenticing with an older photographer to learn the paying craft, and I went to as many exhibits as I could in my off hours. Anything involving a Group *f*/64 member, I would attend without fail. I think I had aspirations of joining the Group.

"But over time, I began to wonder if they hadn't maybe gone a step or two overboard. Obviously they'd developed the art and gotten it to mature to a level it had never reached before. But I began to wonder whether, in their drive for technical purity, they weren't maybe factoring out the human touch completely. So I started consciously messing with the formula. Instead of pristine compositions, I'd make sure to include evidence that people had just recently passed through the scene: fingerprints, wear marks, trails, artifacts, other things like that. And I'd sometimes allow parts of the frame to drop out, either in focus or in exposure, to redirect the viewer's attention to the places where I wanted them to pay attention. The idea was to combine the modernists' precision with the pictorialists' sense of drama and rhetoric.

"I had a few shows and sold some prints—not many, but a few. And let me tell you, I heard it from some of the critics who dropped by. 'Recidivism' was probably the kindest thing that sort of critic said. But there were also some who seemed to get what I was doing."

Wheeler's presentation concluded with the Devil's Tower image from his office projected on the screen. "So there was a depression, and a war, and a few other things. I ended up moving out here and spending more time just being a working photographer. But I still had all of my equipment, and over the years, I've continued to sneak some creative work in. And I'll be having one more exhibition. It'll be here, on campus, starting in August, and it'll run through October. So the prints will be on display for the first few weeks of the fall term. I'd be grateful if you'd drop by."

Wheeler paused for a moment. "Lot of talking, I'm afraid. Sorry about that. Any questions? Yes, sir."

A teenage boy stood up and addressed Wheeler. "If someone asked you to prove that photography was really art, what would you tell them?"

Wheeler grinned at him. "I'd propose an experiment. Get ten identical cameras and round up ten young artists. Then hand one camera to each of the artists and give them instructions to take the most creative photograph they could of the same subject. After the artists came back and all of the film was developed, you'd have ten completely different photographs that showed you ten completely different perceptions, or experiences, of the subject—not ten identical photos. It would be just the same sort of result as you'd get if you asked the artists to paint a picture of the subject, or create a sculpture. I guess that would be an experimental way of scientifically detecting the presence of art. Yes, ma'am."

A young woman stood up. "So you knew the Group *f*/64 photographers personally?"

Wheeler waggled his head. "I didn't 'know them personally,' exactly. It's probably more accurate to say that I crossed paths with several of them. Yes, sir."

A young man followed up the first question. "Can you tell us anything about your experiences of them? What were they like?"

Wheeler stroked his mustache and thought for a moment. "That's kind of tough. I remember Imogen Cunningham as being very inquisitive, and having a great memory of and curiosity about all kinds of technical details. Adams, of course, was outspoken, gregarious, and even funny, but he tended to exert his own gravitational field even back then. Weston had such a reputation by the time I met him that it was hard for me to gauge him personally. He seemed very serious, a very deep thinker, almost ascetic. But that may have just been the face he put on for us younger guys. Yes, sir, in the back."

"You've been showing us mostly landscapes and still lifes this evening," a middle-aged man said. "Has that been your typical mix of subjects?"

"Mostly, but not exactly," Wheeler said. "Of course, if you go up into the north-central part of the state, lots of people know me only as the guy who takes their senior portraits in high school. But I like portraiture in a larger sense. Every so often, if I can do it, I'll do a full portrait study of someone, the sort that actually reflects artistic discipline and tells a story about its subject. I'm hoping to have at least a couple of those in the exhibition. Ma'am?"

"Have you ever considered working in color?"

Wheeler nodded. "That's a funny thing. Most of us older folks grew up with black and white and have found color a bit restrictive. But that's probably a combination of our own age and color having started later, so wasn't as flexible for a while. A lot of older photographers pooh-poohed color because it was 'too literal'—which is funny because after Group *f*/64, everyone was trying to get more literal, in a sense, even in black and white.

"More to your point, I obviously use color in my day-to-day work all the time. And since I turned up in the press, I've been looking into the dye-transfer process for creative work. It's a pain in the ass—sorry, everybody—but it does give you some of the extra control that we old folks are hoping for. Yes, sir."

A younger man stood up. "Have you ever done any figure work?"

Wheeler gave him a long look. "Nudes, you mean?" The man nodded. "Well, most of the photographic artists back when I started were doing at least some. Not Adams, that I know of, but many of the others. The technical challenges are intriguing. So I did a few. Not many." He smiled. "I never really had the knack for 'interviewing' models for that sort of thing the way some of 'em used to." There was a small wave of embarrassed laughter from the room. "Yes, ma'am?"

A woman in her thirties spoke. "There has been some information going around that you had to leave the artistic side of your business after a divorce. Can you address that?"

After the long day's drive and Wheeler's lecture, Janice's mind had gone adrift. Her attention suddenly snapped back to the discussion.

A man sitting in the front row stood up and began to address the woman. "Ma'am, personal questions are not appropriate for this lecture ..."

Wheeler cut him off. "It's okay, Dan. Side effect of my new notoriety, probably. So I'll deal with it." He addressed the woman directly. "The answer is yes. As I say, several things converged at about the same time. But the terms of the divorce included the usual obligations—alimony and child support—plus sixty-seven percent of any proceeds from sales of photographic art of any kind. With that, and particularly the other shocks to the economy about then, it was impossible for me to continue mounting any kind of exhibitions without losing a lot of money.

"I hoped to get back to showing or selling art if my ex-wife remarried, or if business improved enough for me to try it with the extra constraints in place. But by the time I thought it might work, the market wasn't strong enough. Until now. So now we'll see. One more question ..."

But the woman followed on. Jan listened carefully.

"Is it true that the divorce was on grounds of infidelity?"

The man at the front of the room interrupted her angrily. "That is really out of line, ma'am ..." But Wheeler cut him off again, although he was now returning to the tired, guarded man whom Jan had met the previous summer.

"Dan," he said, "I will have to answer this question sooner or later. It may as well be now." To the woman he said, "The answer is yes." There were quiet murmurs throughout the room. "I would add that at the time, my wife and I were WINOs."

"Excuse me?"

"Wedded in name only." Wheeler explained. That defused the tension in the room somewhat, and there were a few chuckles. "That is not an excuse. It is only an explanation. There are times when there are no happy choices and you must make the least destructive decision you can. I sincerely hope that you never find yourself in such a situation."

Jan found herself both offended and confused. Was he being cavalier here about something that had caused her and her mother so much pain? Or was this simply his way of dealing with the pain on his own side? One way or another, she told herself, she would undoubtedly find out soon.

Wheeler turned his attention back to the room at large. "One more question? An easier one, I hope. Yes, ma'am."

The next question came from a willowy young woman. "Does your work have a message?" she asked.

"I'm not sure that's easier," Wheeler joked. "I've always tried to ferret out beauty wherever I could find it. It seems to me that no matter how painful or ugly life gets, there are always beautiful things, reassuring things, sustaining things, and we need to notice them and honor them to keep the bad stuff from taking over. So that's been my goal, I think. I don't know if I've done that successfully. I also don't know if I've answered your question.

"Please check back when the exhibition opens in the fall, and we'll see. Good night, everybody, and thanks for coming."

The students and other audience members filed out, and Jan approached the front of the room.

"Janice!" Wheeler called out. "Hello, thank you for coming! I can use your help; I want to make sure I put my best foot forward in August."

"Well, I'll do what I can," Jan told him in a reserved voice.

"The Myerses aren't expecting you tonight, are they? You're liable to show up in the wee hours if you try to make it up to Thermop tonight, so they'd be asleep when you got there."

"No, I told them I'd be there tomorrow. I'm staying in a motel down here, and then I'll head up in the morning."

"Okay, good. And you brought your camera?"

"Yep," Jan said. "And I bought a 25A filter and a brick of Tri-X, like you suggested. I've also got my polarizer and some Kodachrome, because I'm not quite so old."

Wheeler laughed. "Got your mailers?"

"Uh-huh."

"Well, great. You should have some time for your own work; I don't expect to be a slavedriver. And you might find more subject matter than you expect."

SIX

Wheeler had arranged for Jan to board with a family he knew during her stay in Thermopolis. Among other things, regardless of how strained their family ties were, his studio took up the rooms that he would otherwise have used in putting up a visitor.

The Myers family lived in a big, old frame house on the outskirts of town, with a chain-link fence and an actual grass lawn. A willow and a cottonwood near the house provided cover and shade. Jan stepped onto the porch and rang the doorbell.

A short, plump, prematurely white-haired woman answered. "You must be Janice!" she said. "Welcome, come in! Was your drive all right?"

"It wasn't too bad," Jan said. "Long, of course."

"Well, yes," Mrs. Myers said. All the way from San Francisco, wasn't it?"

"Yeah." Jan smiled.

"Well, I hope you'll be comfortable with us while you're here helping Jim. Our eldest three have grown up and moved out, so it isn't the madhouse it used to be. Your room is upstairs and all the way to one end. This way. You can call me Jenny, by the way."

"Pleased to meet you, Jenny. I usually go by Jan."

Jenny had set aside a bedroom previously used by one of her now-grown children. A small bathroom shared by those children now served as the guest bathroom. After Jenny showed her in, Jan brought in her suitcases and camera bag, set them in a corner, and breathed deeply. In the comfortable, homely surroundings and with the driving done, she could feel tension flowing out of her. A warm, sage-scented breeze outside stirred the cottonwood branches and snuck under the raised window. In the distance a meadowlark sang.

Jan gave a final sigh of contentment and began to unpack.

"It's no trouble at all, believe me," Jenny's husband Greg said at dinner that night. "With three kids off on their own we've got plenty of space, and we're happy to do Jim a favor."

As with the rest of the Myers house, the dining room and its contents seemed a size or two too large. The parents sat with Jan at one end of a massive mahogany table, while two teenagers—a boy and a girl—tinkered with their meals a few feet away.

"Are you friends of his?" Jan asked.

Everything about Greg seemed rough-hewn. He ran a slab-sized hand over his square jaw. "Well, we've known Jim for years," he said. "He's not the most outgoing person I've ever met, but he's done all of our school portraits—fantastic work." Greg paused. "Of course, with all of the latest news, that last part doesn't seem as remarkable as it used to," he said.

"It seems strange, Jim being an artist in San Francisco all of those years ago," Jenny said. "From what Jim told us, he had no idea that people were buying up his artwork until you told him."

Jan gave a lopsided smile. "That's true. My Art History instructor had picked up the story and told me. So last year I came out here to see if I could find him."

"You didn't know him before?"

"No, the family was ..." Jan paused for a moment. "I'd say 'estranged.'"

"Well, that's an awful shame." Jenny looked confused. "But he's always worked as a photographer out here. What kind of art did he do out there?"

"Photographic art, dear," Greg said.

"Well, I guess I'm a little confused," Jenny responded. "I mean, there are the pictures that we take around the house, and the portraits that Jim does of our kids, but that's not the same as *artwork,* is it?"

"Well, what about painted portraits, dear?"

"That's different," Jenny said. "Someone spent days and weeks with a paintbrush putting them together."

Jan cut in. "To make a really fine photograph is a bit different from taking film to a lab. You usually go through several tries before you get it just so. Sometimes you have to add or subtract light in places ..."

"How do you do that?"

"Usually with pieces of paper with holes in them, or little tools that you use to cast a shadow." Jan pantomimed small circular movements with her hands. Jenny just shook her head.

"I'm helping Jim make new prints for his exhibit at the University this fall," Jan continued. "I hope he arranges a show here, too. That would probably make more sense than me trying to explain it."

Greg spoke again. "There was all that work that Jim did for Bertie last year, remember, dear?" In an aside to Jan, he said, "Bertie's our oldest. He works for the Forest Service, and he was trying to keep a mountainside from being stripmined. The mining company didn't really need to dig there; they had plenty of diggings in other places around the state. So Bertie talked it over with Jim, and the two of them went off to document their case.

"While they were out there, Jim did a few pictures to show how pretty the area was. Some of them were mighty impressive." Greg smiled. "He even did a couple in black-and-white that looked like you could reach into 'em. We ought to talk to Bertie and see if he still has any of them, dear."

"There's a long tradition of that kind of work, using photographs to argue against unnecessary development," Jan said. "Jim hasn't mentioned that he was doing any of it, though."

"I'm not too much of a hippie on these things," Greg said. "Nothing wrong with honest business, and a lot of people benefit from it. But Bertie and Jim are both dead set that this particular company is trouble."

"What company is it?" Jan asked.

"CGM," Greg answered. "Chambers Group Minerals."

"Never heard of them."

"Well, you could probably find out more when you head back home. Their headquarters is out near San Francisco somewhere."

INTERLUDE: 1939

Jim whistled his way through his morning routine, shaving and brushing his hair in great high spirits. (He did, however, have to interrupt his whistling to brush his teeth.)

He strode confidently through his living room and into the kitchen, where Dora was tidying up.

"Good morning, Dora dear! Gimme a kiss!"

Dora held out one soapy, wrinkled palm to his face. "Try it and you'll get slapped. What the hell is with you, anyway?"

"Oh, not much," said Jim with a sly grin. "I just landed a deal that puts us well into the black, that's all."

"So what? If you'd gone into some normal line of work, it wouldn't have taken us this long." Dora pushed an errant blonde curl away from her right temple. "What's this big deal, then?"

"I've signed a contract to provide all of the photographs for the advertising and promotions of Chambers Industries."

"Chambers? The real estate company?"

"That's their oldest business, yes. But they've also branched out into manufacturing. So far, they're mainly subcontracting to car companies. But they've got a lot of production lines to cover in their ads and their annual reports. And best of all, they're loaded."

"Financially, not alcoholically."

Jim snorted. "Yes, that's what I meant. Listen, we've been invited to a party the company's throwing on Saturday night. They've reached some sort of money target, so they're throwing a big bash."

Dora looked alarmed. "Saturday's my bridge night! You know that."

"I know, and I'm sorry. But the company keeps its own schedule. It's important for me to be there, and it would be a big boost if you were there with me. I'm going to try to collar the owner—Mr. Frank Chambers, himself."

For the first time that morning, and actually in some time previously, Jim had said something that had impressed his wife. "Well, all right," she said, surprised. "I'll let the girls know. What time should I be ready?"

"It starts at six, so we should be out of here by five."

"Five it is. And I assume you're off to work now. Are you starting on Chambers' work today?"

"I start their project next week, actually. Today I'm finishing up shooting for my latest project for Capwell's."

"So one of those tramps you work with is coming in."

Jim's initial morning euphoria was ebbing quickly. "Dear," he said through his teeth, "all of the models who come in are professionals."

"Well, that's what I just said."

"Managed by talent agencies, not pimps or madames. Try to discuss the situation like an adult, please."

In complete fairness to Dora, not all of the models who came to Jim's studio had the same levels of cooperation and initiative. None were as Dora described them, but not all were quite up to Jim's rejoinders, either.

Because of that, and after the morning's harangue, Jim was relieved to be working with Zoë Quinlan that day. Zoë was always on time, worked efficiently despite her admittedly amusing banter, and was continually constructive. Jim was coming to the point of considering Zoë to be a friend as well as a model.

She was also, Jim admitted to himself, as cute as the proverbial button—not that that was a particularly rare trait among models, but it always helped.

At nine on the dot, there was the usual brisk knock at the door. Jim opened it and let Zoë in.

"Hey, Zoë, how've things been?"

"About the same, thanks. Well, what do we have today? Necklaces and earrings?"

"That's right. Just as we discussed on the phone. That's why I asked you to wear an outfit with a blouse, rather than a full dress."

She looked at him with her flashing dark eyes, one eyebrow raised slightly. "You know, I don't think I've ever worn a necklace or a pair of earrings below the beltline."

"No, I imagine not. But I arranged with Capwell's to loan us some dressy blouses for use as costume. We could put yours in a shot or two as well, if you like."

"That's okay. I might get recognized. Is the box in the changing room?"

"Just outside."

Zoë put on the first "costume" blouse with a necklace and a pair of earrings, then reported to her usual spot in front of the camera. "Ready for the oven!" she called.

"Okay, broiler on!"

"Ow," Zoë said, looking at the floor for a moment. Jim had activated the lights too quickly and caught her looking toward one of them. "Well, you seem pretty chipper today."

"Yeah, it hasn't been too bad."

"How are things at home?"

"About the same."

While Jim made his preliminary adjustments, Zoë shrugged. "I'm sorry to hear that," she said.

"Well, I may have made a dent in the armor. In any case, I'll have a bit more flexibility. Maybe I can risk some creative work." He told Zoë about his latest deal.

To his surprise, Zoë looked apprehensive. "Chambers?" she asked. "Not Frank Chambers?"

"Actually, yes. I haven't met him personally, I've been dealing with his marketing deputy. But I'm hoping to introduce myself to him at a function his company is hosting this weekend."

Zoë lowered her eyes for a moment. At first Jim thought she was still trying to rid them of glare, but then she looked back up at him.

"Be very careful, Jim," Zoë said.

"Why?"

"I don't have any first-hand knowledge," she continued, "but I've heard some things. One of my friends rented a place from him. She describes him, at different times, as an ass and a snake."

"Zoologically confused, then."

"I'm serious, Jim. Another friend of mine worked in one of his companies and you don't even want to know the details."

That finally caught Jim's attention. "All right, I'll keep an eye on him."

"You'd better," Zoë told him. "I don't want you getting hurt."

Jim gave an embarrassed smile. "Gosh, and I didn't think you cared."

Zoë's expression was now completely unsuitable for the morning's work. She paused, then shook her head. "My God," she said, her voice tense with emotion.

"Hey, hey ..." Jim was suddenly conscious of his failure to track something in the conversation, although he wasn't yet sure what it was. "I'm sorry. I thought we were just throwing our usual brickbats at each other. I didn't mean to make you angry, Zoë."

She pulled herself back together. "It's all right. But I'm worried for you. I'm telling you, I've heard he's tricky and dangerous. And I really don't want you to be hurt."

Jim looked down, then back at those dark eyes. "It's good to have people looking out for you. I'll just leave it there for now. And now I've made you have to go back and fix your hair. I apologize."

The ballroom where Chambers Industries was throwing its party was built in the days before the stock market crash. When it was new, it represented the muscle of the new money arising all around the country. Now, in the aftermath of the crash, with the lucky ones outside scratching to keep the bills paid, it seemed garish and tasteless.

The Wheelers entered through geometrically ornamented brass doors. After descending a massive piano-black Art Deco staircase, they began to work their way across the floor. Somewhere in the distance a jazz band was playing softly. At the moment, they were providing background music; their heavier barrages would come later.

Jim looked sideways at Dora and smiled. In her flowing bronze-colored dress and blonde pincurls, looking ahead with her cool, incisive expression, she cut an impressive figure. "You've really outdone yourself tonight," he told her. "Thank you."

"I'll try to keep that in mind when I have to go to the john," she responded. "Seriously, you don't have to wear this thing."

"Noted," Jim said through his teeth. He motioned to a balding man at the far end of the room. "Oh, look, there's Martin."

"That's not Chambers, is it?"

"No. Martin is his marketing man—the fellow who offered me the contract."

Martin stepped up to a podium and made a gesture off to one side. "Hello, is this on?" he asked in a low, droning voice. "Oh, thanks. Everybody, could I have your attention for a minute? Attention please!" The partygoers turned around and listened.

"I'm Martin Pettibone, Vice President and Director of Marketing for Chambers Industries. Thank you for coming. Are you enjoying yourselves?" There was a roar of approval.

"Well, there's plenty to celebrate tonight. Chambers Industries announced its financial results today, and we were able to report a ten-percent increase in profit!" The partygoers cheered. "I'm pleased to tell you that both divisions did great. Our profits still came mainly from the Real Estate division, which is mighty amazing in these times, but the new machining and manufacturing division is coming up fast.

"Ladies and gentlemen," he concluded, "there is no depression within these walls!" The partygoers cheered again, louder this time.

"And now," Martin said, "let me turn over the microphone to the man who makes this all possible, the captain of our corporate ship. Ladies and gentlemen, I present the President of Chambers Industries, Mr. Frank Chambers!"

The room erupted in applause as Chambers ascended the podium. His jet-black hair was swept neatly back and his bespoke double-breasted jacket carried no wrinkles or sags. He was, simply put, a man composed entirely of straight, sharp edges.

"Good evening, everyone," Chambers began in a clear, measured baritone voice. "Martin is in charge of marketing, so I'll leave the flights of rhetoric to him. I do second his sentiments, though. In these times, we have to invest not only time and effort, but also care, to keep the company on a secure footing. And many people here have been making that investment. The folks in Finance and Accounting," he waved toward a group of women clustered together like turkeys in a thunderstorm, "have been piling on the coal to collect and save every penny they can. The Machining and Manufacturing team has really stepped up this year, turning its first profit since we started it three years ago. And of course, Real Estate has continued to be our engine, with our investment managers finding the growth in the market and our rental agents pounding the pavement to keep the cashflow running smoothly.

"The whole list is too long for me to read off," Chambers said with a slight smile. "But please rest assured that I value your contribution regardless of where you are in the company or what you do. It's all critical to our success. That's why I pay you for it."

There was a nervous chuckle from the floor.

"Well, I'll let you get back to the celebration. Thank you for your time, thank you for your efforts, and back to the grind on Monday!"

The music began again, and Jim wound his way through the crowd with Dora on his arm. "Martin!" he called.

Martin turned around slowly. "Jim, glad you could come!" he said. "Of course, you're just starting to work with us, but I'm expecting great things." He turned to Dora. "And you must be Mrs. Wheeler."

"Yes," Dora said in a convincing impersonation of demureness and decorum. "Charmed, I'm sure, Mr. Pettibone."

"The pleasure's mine," Martin said. "Uh, Jim, would you be willing to hang in for a moment? I'd like to see if I can flag Frank down to meet you. Just a minute ..." Martin waved wildly in the direction of a corner of the room, and in a minute or two, the hard-edged profile of the corporate president could be seen wading toward them through the crowd.

"Frank," Martin said, "allow me to introduce Jim Wheeler and his wife ..."

"Dora," said Dora, with an embarrassed look on her face.

"I've just signed Jim to do the photographic work for our corporate publications," Martin finished lamely.

Chambers' eyebrows raised slightly. Otherwise, his expression did not change. "Oh, yes," he said. "Martin showed me the portfolio you left with him. Very impressive. But at first, I thought you'd invited one of your models to the party tonight. Unless you do double duty, my dear?"

Dora regarded Chambers with a coquettishly disapproving expression. "No, of course not," she said. "I don't even go to his office that often."

Chambers turned back to her husband. “I don’t know about this, Jim,” he said. “Bad business, not exploiting a resource like that.” He winked at Dora, who retreated back to her stance of false disapproval. “Just joking, of course. Good to meet you both, and Jim, welcome aboard.” With that, he waded away in the direction he had come.

Martin appeared to have vanished while Chambers was speaking. Jim took a deep breath and relaxed, then turned toward his wife. “Well, shall we go over to the buffet and grab something for dinner?” he asked.

But Dora was appraising him intently, and her new expression was impossible to read.

SEVEN

When Jan knocked on Wheeler's front door, he was waiting for her. "Come in, come in!" he said cheerfully. "Welcome back."

"Thank you for giving me the opportunity," Jan said. "I know the visit last year was strange, and I appreciate a chance to clear things up."

"Nah, don't mention it." Wheeler dismissed her concerns with a wave of one hand. "Anyway, the news you brought me has done all kinds of good. Along with setting up the exhibit, the University helped me get a grant so that I could prepare the artwork that will be on display. So I've got a couple of fresh six-by-seven Pentaxes, and not a moment too soon. The two I had were on their last legs. And I've had the large format shutters overhauled, too. Plus, the grant brought in enough to pay a darkroom assistant. And here you are."

"So," Jan asked, "where do I begin?"

"We'll spend the first few days in the darkroom, so I can show you how my process works. I've picked out the negatives I want to print for the show, and I've put them all into a list that's currently on my desk. We'll start with the easiest ones, and then I'll need you to do the printing for the rest of the negatives on the list.

"That's the easy part. After that, we put on rubber gloves and aprons and tone the prints, and then we get to scrunch down with single-haired brushes and spot them."

"Do you think we're going to have enough time?"

"If we're careful. But as I say, I'm not trying to be a slave-driver here. You should have time enough to get out, look the place over, and shoot anything that seems to call for it. And as for me, I'm going to need to take a couple of road trips to print things I can't do here."

"Such as?"

"Specialty items," Wheeler said. "I have six eight-by-ten negatives that are not on the list, because I'm printing them oversize. To do that, I need an eight-by-ten enlarger, which I don't have here."

"But you used one to make *that*, right?" Jan motioned toward the enormous photograph of Devil's Tower.

"Exactly. The prints I'm making this month aren't that big; they'll be about four times normal. And I have two images that should get people talking." Wheeler motioned across his imaginary marquée. "Old man creates color photograph. Read all about it."

"You *must* have a color enlarger here for your portrait work. Don't you?"

"Sure," Wheeler gave one of his grins. "But these are shot on eight-by-ten color sheets, and they'll be dye-transfer printed. As I said the other night, it's a nuisance, but it gives you at least a bit of a handle on the final image."

He walked to his desk and pulled out the center tray, then pulled out two keys on a fob. "While you are working with me," he said, "these will be available here in the desk. One of them opens the storage closet in the hallway between here and the studio room, and the other one opens the topmost cabinet in the closet. That cabinet contains my personal negative files. Come this way."

In the closet, Wheeler opened the upper cabinet to reveal a row of binders. At the right end of the row was a space wide enough for about three binders. He drew out a binder at the left end and flipped it open. "Okay, let's head back to the desk," he said.

Once there, he flipped through the binder to a specific point, then turned it around and slid it across the desk toward Jan. On one side, the binder was open to a manila tab with a number written on it. A black-and-white print was taped to the tab. Opposite it was a neatly folded, transparent sleeve.

"Do not remove the negative yet, please," Wheeler said. "Not until we're actually in the darkroom. And *never* slide it out of the sleeve. These sleeves open up from the inside, to prevent scratches. But there's no need to expose it to risk of damage yet. One other thing: see the little Z in the number?" Jan nodded. "This is a Zone System negative, so it shouldn't need so much jiggering in the darkroom. Let's head down."

But just as the two had reached their feet, a knock sounded at the door. Wheeler stepped to the door and opened it.

"Carol Bradford!" Jan heard Wheeler exclaim. "It's good to see you, young lady. How can I help you?"

Past Wheeler, Jan could just barely hear Carol's quiet, nervous voice. "I came to see if you could do something for me."

"Well, step inside," Wheeler said. "We can go over it sitting down."

The woman attached to the voice was tall and broad-shouldered. Jan figured her as being in her early twenties. Wheeler motioned her to the empty chair facing his desk and sat down in his own chair on the other side. She sat next to Jan for a moment, facing him, but worrying her lower lip with her teeth.

“Are you all right?” Wheeler asked her.

“Yes, thanks,” Carol said.

Wheeler tried to draw her out a little. “How’s your young man? Stephen, right?”

“Right. You knew we were engaged, didn’t you?”

“So I heard. Congratulations, by the way! And I’ve seen Steve on patrol, so I assume he’s all done with his academy training, right?”

“That’s right,” Carol said with a smile.

“When’s the wedding?”

“September fifteenth.”

Wheeler did a double-take. “You’re not here to ask me to cover the wedding, are you?” he asked. “I’m too heavily booked on a special project. Plus, it’s a little bit late for me to start getting ready for something that big.”

“No, Mr. Wheeler. I’m only looking for a single picture. I want a portrait done for my husband—one that he can always look at and see what I looked like when he married me.”

“I would be honored.”

“And I want it to be ...” Carol threw an embarrassed sidelong glance in Jan’s direction. “... not completely polite.”

“Oh.” Wheeler suddenly seemed to be at a loss for words. “So ... a portrait with a little something extra added.”

“You could say that,” Carol said, looking sideways at Jan once again.

“You know, if you ducked into one of the towns down south for an afternoon, some place big enough for a shopping mall, they have studios that specialize in portraits with a little something extra added. ‘Boudoir photography,’ I think they call it.”

Carol shook her head. "No, I've looked at them, and the examples they had were kind of tacky-looking. I want something for Steve to keep, so it ought to be worth keeping."

Wheeler regarded Carol for at least five seconds. Finally he asked, "Why come to me?"

"There have been rumors going around," Carol said. "Is it true that you had a studio out on the West Coast when you were younger?"

"True enough."

"And you exhibited your work?"

"I had a few shows—two or three," Wheeler said quietly. "Not that many."

"So that's why," Carol said. "Most of us in this town have been doing business with you for years, and we always felt lucky to have you. Now that I have a better idea about why we did, I also think that you would be the best person to do this portrait the way I want it done."

"Well," Wheeler said, "I certainly haven't done anything this far out of the ordinary portrait work in many years. And one way or another, I've never had to field a question like this from one of my neighbors."

Carol buried her face in her hands. "I know."

Wheeler took a deep breath. "Okay, I've skipped a step, first of all," he said, motioning toward Jan. "This is Janice Gibson."

"Jan."

"Pleased to meet you."

"Jan has come out from San Francisco to help me get ready for a new exhibit," Wheeler continued. "It opens the first week in August, down at the university in Laramie. We're expecting good turnout. So it seems my past is finally catching up with me."

"Now as far as what you've asked me to do, I could do it for you. But there are ground rules, and things you need to consider."

Carol nodded. "Go ahead."

"The first thing is that this will be an expensive photograph. As I say, this is not the sort of thing I normally do. But if I'm going to do it, I'm not cutting corners. That means there will be a lot of handcrafting, a lot of moving and changing lights, cameras, furniture, props if we have any, and you. There will also be hair and makeup work involved. Got it?"

"Got it."

"You'll have a formal estimate before we start. The second thing is that each one of us will have to have a second with us—someone who can observe the proceedings and bear witness that everything is on the up-and-up. Yours should be someone you trust."

"Is that necessary?" Carol asked.

"Yes, it is," Wheeler said. "One approach we could take would be a waist-up portrait that's basically all hints. The effect would be something like this." He folded his arms low over his chest, leaned toward Carol, and batted his eyelashes at her. She laughed in response.

"The problem is, for us to get that picture, you're going to have to be a bit less discreet than that where *I* can see you," Wheeler continued. "You will have to shift around between takes, and I'll be directing a little during that time. I can't do that with my eyes closed. So we'll all have to know that if you say, "We're done," at any point, we all turn around and walk away from it. Our seconds make sure that it happens, that everyone is comfortable with the whole process, and that no one's arm was twisted at any time. Literally or figuratively," Wheeler amended himself. "On the other hand, if you decide you're comfortable improvising, having witnesses helps confirm that everything remained voluntary at all times.

"You know Kate, right? The lady with the nail studio and gift shop north of downtown? She'll be my second for this. She'll also double as our hair and makeup person. That's if she agrees to it—I'll have to ask her—but I expect she'll be willing to help. If not, we'll regroup.

"And there will be legal paperwork for all four of us to sign. Still okay?"

Carol nodded slowly. "You don't always do all of this for a portrait session."

"But not all sessions are like this one is going to be," Wheeler said. "Even for a regular session there's a short waiver, but for this, everything has to be defined clearly.

"All right, next item. I will not be using any diffusion filters or soft focus. Given our discussion a few minutes ago, I assume that's okay." Carol nodded and Wheeler continued. "I have a substitute—an improvement, really—that I think you'll like. As with all shoots, I keep the negatives.

"So how are you so far? Scared yet?"

"A little," Carol said. "Not quite scared off."

"There's one last thing that may do it," Wheeler told her. "You have to understand—and you have to be absolutely clear before the shoot, if you decide to proceed—that what you are doing here is insanely dangerous. You are putting a compromising image of yourself into the hands of a man who may use it against you."

Carol shook her head slowly. "But Steve would never do such a thing. I know that from the bottom of my heart."

"That may not be good enough," Wheeler said. "You are a bride-to-be. So, unless you're also a complete cynic, you're inclined to give him way too much of the benefit of the doubt.

But once you let this out of the bag, you can't get it back. He can show it to his buddies, pin it to the bulletin board at the station, anything he wants."

Carol's voice was quiet again. "I can't imagine him doing any of those things."

Wheeler leaned over the desk. "I am asking you to take all of this home with you and think about it, hard. Sleep on it. Ask yourself whether it's worth it. If you still decide to go ahead with it, call or drop back by and let me know. Okay?"

"Okay," Carol said. "I'd better go. I'll let you know within two or three days. Thanks, Mr. Wheeler."

After shutting and locking the door behind Carol, Wheeler turned his attention back to Jan. "Well, that was unexpected," he said, exhaling dramatically afterward. "What a day!"

"May I ask you something?" Jan said.

"Sure. What?"

"That conversation was obviously really awkward, for both of you. Why didn't you just say no?"

Wheeler took another deep breath. "I think my answer has to have a couple of layers to it," he said. "The surface layer is that she's right about those 'boudoir' guys. They're doing pretty crude work, a lot of them. Some of them may find their depth eventually, but for right now, that's the state of things.

"The other layer is ambition—hopefully not ego, but definitely a bit of ambition. I think I could potentially be of help to her, and I would be willing to try, as long as everyone plays fair and the situation remains as safe as possible. If Carol is willing to work with me on this, and if we are all careful enough, it could work to everyone's benefit."

Wheeler picked up the receiver of the telephone on the desk and dialed—*zzip, zzzzzzzzip, zzzzip*. After greeting Kate, he spent about five minutes summarizing Carol's visit.

"Okay, thanks. Do you know of anyone who might be able to get us a read on young Steve Paulson, Carol's fiancé? I really have doubts about Carol's objectivity right now. Thanks again.

"Yeah, Jan's here. I was just about to get her started in the darkroom when Carol showed up. Oh, and that reminds me. I need to ask you something about the exhibit, but I'll talk to you in person about that. Just ask if I forget—yeah, I know, I know. Talk to you soon. G'bye."

Wheeler turned back to Jan. "And now, finally," he said, "let's get downstairs before something else interrupts us." He walked past the storage closet and opened a narrow door behind it. "Right down here. Watch your head." He took a deep breath of the musty air drifting up the steep stairway. "Ah, I love the smell of hypo in the morning!"

The first day's work was exhausting, but by the end of it, Jan felt she was beginning to find her way fairly well, and she hadn't committed any major blunders in technique or darkroom hygiene. The following day, Jan and Wheeler interrupted their training long enough for a quick lunch out.

They rode down the main street in Wheeler's weathered Ford pickup, scanning the surroundings for signs of a county sheriff's patrol car. When they saw one standing outside a fast food restaurant, they stopped there as well and headed in.

The two of them had discussed a plan while still working in Wheeler's darkroom, and they now put it into play. Tall and broad-shouldered, Steve Paulson cut an impressive figure, particularly while in uniform. Wheeler slipped in behind him while Jan leaned over a railing and studied the menu for a moment.

When the young man behind the counter turned to take the next order, Jan ducked under the railing, cut in front of Paulson, and submitted her order first. She then turned to face him, as though noticing him for the first time.

"Oh, was there a line?" she asked in an innocent voice. "I'm sorry, I didn't know."

Paulson stewed for a few minutes, but he had begun to cool down by the time the young man was ready to turn back for another order. Before he could do so, Wheeler muttered something under his breath.

"Women!" he said. "Can't live with 'em, can't shoot 'em!"

Paulson turned briefly around and pinned Wheeler in a momentary expression of withering disgust before turning back and submitting his order.

On the way back to his studio, Wheeler thanked Jan for her help. "He checks out so far. We'll see if Kate can come up with any dirt. If not, and if Carol wants to proceed, it looks like I'm in for it." He raised one eyebrow. "If you see Carol, could you fill her in? I suspect that if I'm invited to the wedding, I'll have to sit on the bride's side now, but I'd at least like her to know what this was about in case he mentions it to her."

INTERLUDE: 1940

Zoë stood in front of a gray velvet backdrop, clad in a sensible-looking knee-length dress. She gripped a matching leather clutch in her left hand while she rested her right hand on her hip.

"Hold still," Jim said from behind the camera. "Hold it ... hold it ... great! Thanks."

He stood up slowly, bolstering his back with his hands and groaning slightly. "Ugh. I think I've been crouching back there most of my waking hours recently."

"Yes, pretty soon you'll be welded in," Zoë said. "How has the Chambers thing been going?"

"Busy, really busy. I must have been to fifty sites or so in the last month, and that's meant a lot of darkroom work too. But business is looking up, so I can't complain."

"Sure you can. Nobody will listen to you, that's all." Zoë shifted topics. "Thanks for the extra money, by the way. It comes in awfully handy."

"Glad to do it," Jim said with a smile. "You've been a mainstay for me, a real rock. And I appreciate it more than I can tell you."

"Aw, shucks. I thought you just kept calling me back for the insults."

"Well, those too. Seriously, though, it's no trouble. I'm meeting budget, coming in a little over. Things are nice and stable here, and at home, too."

Zoë's expression became oddly muted. "Things improving between you and your wife?" she asked.

"Yeah. Apparently not scrimping so hard helps."

"That's good to hear," Zoë said quietly. "I'm glad for you."

Jim looked at her. "Are you all right?"

"I'm fine. Just tired." Zoë looked up and smiled. "If we don't have any more material to shoot today, I'd better get back into my own clothes and head home. It's getting late."

"Oh, sorry. I didn't mean to keep you."

"No trouble at all. But it would be good to get home before it's too dark."

Jim waited in his office while Zoë changed, then helped her into her coat and saw her to the door, as always. As she walked away down the sidewalk, something seemed different about her; her normal, brisk, clicking gait was changed. Now she walked away—just walked.

He returned to his desk and pulled a manila folder out of a stack. From the folder he withdrew a dozen prints, which he scattered on his desktop. He studied each of them intently, sometimes brushing at one with a fingertip. Occasionally, he bent over a print, peering through a large loupe at tiny details. After several minutes of this scrutiny, he picked up one print and put it into a wire tray to his right. He repeated this process with nine additional folders; when he was done, the wire basket contained ten selected prints. These he placed into a large envelope, which he sealed and set dead center on the desktop. That should be enough, he thought, to remind him to call a courier first thing in the morning and get the selections over to Martin right away. Then he could start developing what he and Zoë had just shot for Capwell's.

Jim locked up his office and headed home. "Hi, honey, it's me!" he said when he opened his front door.

"Hello, darling," he heard Dora say in the distance. "You're a bit late. Busy day today?"

He walked into the living room as Dora arrived from the back of their flat. Her lively expression and inquisitive eyes reminded him of when they first met. Back then, she had shown him an enigmatic mixture of interest and evasion, and he had devoted himself over the next year or two to winning her over. Since then, he had often had cause to wonder whether he should have paid more attention to the value of the prize before he made his bid. But then, he had been young at the time.

And in any case, that appeared to be water under the bridge now.

"Hi there," he repeated, now that he could see Dora and there was no need to shout. "Yeah, there was a lot to do. The good news is that I've finished the first run of shoots for Chambers Industries. They should have all the material they need now to finish their annual report. I'm sending the last batch to Martin first thing in the morning."

"Excellent," Dora said. "And they seem happy with the work?"

"Better than happy. I haven't even been asked for any retakes."

"Well, looks like someone in the organization is looking out for you, then."

"And I just finished shooting for Capwell's, late this afternoon. I'll develop and print over the next couple of days, and then they'll be up to date, too." He gave a small, derisive snort. "I may have to line up something for Saturday, while you're meeting with your bridge group."

"Oh, I forgot," Dora said. "We've decided to put bridge nights on hold for a little while. Margie is off staying with family out of town for a few months, and the rest of us are going to wait until she comes back."

Besides Dora, Margie was the only member of the group that Jim had ever met. "Oh. So what do you have planned in the meantime?"

Dora beamed at him. "I thought you'd never ask. Well, let's have dinner first, and then I have some exciting news for you."

EIGHT

Jan had been working with Wheeler for two weeks. She felt she could now handle his basic printing demands without too many mistakes. However, she was aware that they were getting close to the end of the more recent, and therefore easier, negatives. Soon, she would have to start dealing with Wheeler's older work—negatives he'd shot years ago, on discontinued film, and printed while creating lab notes for papers and chemistries that were no longer available. At that point, she would have to start recreating the original groundwork as she printed, and she would slow down.

But in the meantime, early summer was still under way. The cool, fresh, dry morning air cheered and invigorated Jan as she walked the short distance from the Myers house to Wheeler's studio.

She let herself in the front door. "Hello!" she called out. "Good morning! It's Jan!"

There was no immediate answer. Jan looked through the office, the storage closet, the studio room, and the darkroom in the basement, but was unable to find Wheeler anywhere. She returned to the main floor and called up the stairs, "Hello? Are you there?"

Suddenly the knob on the back door clattered. The door opened and Wheeler walked in. He was wearing a loose pair of sweatpants and a T-shirt bearing the legend I'M WITH STUPID next to an arrow pointing upward.

"Well, how do I look?" he asked.

"Ridiculous," Jan answered him.

"Perfect," Wheeler pronounced.

Confused, Jan asked, "Why? What's the purpose of looking ridiculous?"

"Young Carol Bradford," Wheeler said. "Kate hasn't been able to flush out any incriminating dirt on Steve Paulson. You may recall that you and I weren't able to trick him into giving anything away, either. He seems to be a modern-day Galahad, from all reports. And Carol has refused to back down. So it looks like I'm doing the shoot this morning, and I need to do whatever I can to avoid making her uneasy."

"Can I help with the shoot?"

"No, I'm afraid this is confidential work," Wheeler told her. "Just Carol, me, and our seconds. The good news for you is you get the day off. Grab your camera and go hunt for compositions, or just look around town a bit. You didn't really have much opportunity when you first got here, I know. But first, I could use some help getting the setup finished." He gave her a sideways look. "When you came out last year, you asked me why I hung on to the greenhouse in the back yard. I told you to figure it out. What did you come up with?"

"Nothing," Jan sighed. "I tried asking Fred about it, and he seems to know, but he wouldn't tell me either."

"Good man!" Wheeler exclaimed. "But I'm sorry that nothing occurred to you. Although it's not a very straightforward idea, not in this day and age. Your instructor gets extra credit if he actually understood. Come this way, please."

Jan followed Wheeler out of the back door and across a narrow, enclosed porch to the door of the greenhouse. He fumbled for his keys and worked one of them in the lock. A second later, he opened the door and showed Jan in.

They were standing in a uniformly white enclosure. Gauzy white fabric wrapped around the enclosure on all sides and hung from wooden racks just under the roof. In one corner, one of the roof racks was withdrawn by about two feet; another rack above it was also retracted and a third remained extended, softening the sunbeam that settled gently into the room. In the midst of all of this stood a sofa draped in pale gray canvas and a variety of reflectors on stands, all of which looked homemade. Two cameras on tripods, one of Wheeler's brand-new medium-format cameras and an ancient view camera, completed the setup.

"Could you grab that reflector over there and aim it toward the center cushion of the sofa?" Wheeler asked, motioning to clarify which reflector he meant. "Thank you."

Jan managed to restrain her curiosity long enough to move the reflector, and the others to which he motioned afterward. Occasionally Wheeler stepped in and moved around the sofa with a lightmeter, taking readings every few inches. Finally he hung the meter on one of the tripods. "That'll do for now," he said. "Thanks again."

Jan looked around herself. Throughout the enclosure, and especially in the area immediately around the sofa, the light was uniform, soft, and pure; everything was clearly visible and nothing hurt the eyes. Even the sunbeam that Wheeler had allowed in was tamed just enough, so that it did not overpower the scene. In the preceding two weeks, Jan had become well acquainted with the qualities of Wyoming summer sunlight: it was clean, but hard. Wheeler had found a way of keeping the purity while blunting the edge.

A knock sounded on the greenhouse door. "Come in!" Wheeler shouted.

Kate entered first. She nodded curtly at Jan and waved in Wheeler's direction. After her, Carol and another young woman entered. Carol was wearing understated makeup and her strawberry blonde hair was freshly (and rather massively) styled.

"Hi, Jan," Carol said. "This is Michaela. She's been my best friend since second grade, and I was her maid of honor last year." Jan and Michaela greeted each other.

"Now, Carol," Wheeler asked, "did you remember the preparation instructions? Nothing that pinches? Because the pinches will show."

"Don't worry," Kate said. "We went over all of that at my shop before we started on her makeup."

"And one last time," Wheeler repeated, "are you sure you want to proceed with this?"

"Yes, sir."

"Very well, then." Wheeler took a step back and declared, "Welcome to my solar studio! Jan, what do you think, by the way?"

Jan shook her head. "I never would have guessed. And on some level, I think I want one."

"You'd have to build it yourself," Wheeler said. "Otherwise, there's nothing stopping you. Now, Carol, what I'm doing here is modifying the sunlight directly to make it soft and even. The idea is that you get both a nice, smooth rendition and lots of detail at the same time."

"Where on earth did you get the idea?" Carol asked.

"Years ago, I'd read that movie cameras were invented before electric lights, and in the very beginning, they used to shoot their movies in greenhouses that they built as film stages. When I moved here, I saw this house for sale, with its greenhouse, and I figured I'd try to create a studio like that for myself."

He walked to the door and flipped one of a small bank of switches. "I'll turn on the ventilation fan, so that the place doesn't start heating up like a greenhouse—even though that's exactly what it is. Jan, I'll need to ask you to leave now. I don't know how long we're going to be here, so I'm afraid you're on your own for the rest of the day."

Jan bid the group farewell, walked back through Wheeler's studio, and locked the front door behind her. Returning to the Myers house, she chatted with Jenny for a few minutes before changing into her hiking boots, grabbing her camera bag, her tripod, and a broad-brimmed hat, after which she headed out.

The sun was already good and warm, and it was still only mid-morning. The days when the sun would turn enemy and mount its annual attack were not far ahead now. But in the meantime, it remained an ally. It was an excellent day for Carol's shoot, with only a few tiny puffs of cloud on the horizons, and also a good day for Jan to experiment. She walked through the northern part of town, capturing images that seemed inconsequential by themselves, but together—or so she hoped—would create a larger portrait. Weathered old houses; newer light industrial buildings with painted aluminum siding and roofing, themselves already fading with the sun and wind; patterns of cracks in the asphalt on the side streets.

Before the light got too high in the sky, she drove a mile or two east of town and walked off of the dirt road into an adjoining field. Remembering the instructions she'd been given when she arrived, and chuckling a little at her initially horrified reaction, she carefully scanned the ground ahead of her for rattlesnakes as she walked. Greg Myers had explained to her that there weren't really that many of them, and they didn't want trouble with people any more than the people did, but that if you surprised one, it would surprise you back.

Jan found a spot where the nearby hills obscured the town while the nearby road, including her car, was out of her intended field of view. She extended her tripod, bolted down her Nikon, attached both her red filter and her polarizer to the lens, and stopped for a moment.

Sunlight was everywhere.

The scene was nearly silent, punctuated only by a minuscule breeze. Over the stretch of meadow on which Jan stood, golden yellow blades of short wild grass swayed among dry green sage and an occasional Russian thistle. Under the hard blue sky, the grasses danced, reveling in the brief joy of youth in a hard, unforgiving place. In the distance, blankets of green and gold mantled mute red terraces.

It was almost July, and the world was alive.

Jan was not sure how long she simply stood there, breathing deeply and feeling tension drain out of her like water from a bathtub. Without the sounds of human routine—the rhythm of steps, the staccato of speech, the rising hum of automobile traffic, and on and on—Jan's sense of the passage of time went unmoored and unanchored, and simply drifted. Her surroundings buzzed lazily with hidden grasshoppers and every now and then, presumably after eating a loud and unfortunate grasshopper, a meadowlark would voice its signal tone burst. The colors around her, muted and dry though they were, seemed to glow softly under the incandescent sky.

After some indefinite quantity of seconds or minutes, Jan gave a deep, contented sigh and dug into her camera bag. She attached a cable release to the camera, locked its viewing mirror up, and began to shoot.

Later, as she packed everything away again, she stood and thought about where she should go next. The springs were unfortunately problematic because of the tourist crowds, so she headed in a different direction, out past the airport to where Roundtop Mountain loomed over a small, plain cemetery. She shot a few frames of the humble graves with the mountain overshadowing them, then moved her car to a small loop where she could park at the mountain's base.

Roundtop Mountain seemed to be the victim of an identity crisis; it could not make up its mind whether it wanted to be a mountain, a hill, a mesa, a volcano, or some of each. Its brilliant red slopes spread out in sharp folds and ridges to form a truncated cone, at whose top was a layer of crumbling white rock.

A trail from the loop zigzagged toward the top. Jan grabbed her camera and left the tripod behind, and then trudged and scrambled her way upward. A few minutes later, panting from the dryness and perhaps a bit of altitude, she pulled herself up onto the surface of the mesa.

By and large, to live in the West is to work, eat, and sleep amid the marks of unimaginable planetary violence. There is always a scar or a wound close at hand—the upended fossil seabeds of the Colorado Front Range, the San Andreas Fault in California, the volcanoes in the Pacific Northwest, the obsidian fields in Oregon, and on and on. But in Northwest Wyoming, at whose edge Thermopolis stands, the grand sweep of the land bears testimony to eons of pressure and heat—forces that remained just below the surface, providing power to the displays in Yellowstone and the Thermopolis hot springs alike, forever threatening to renew its assault. Enormous bands of stone lie in twisted waves across the landscape, rippling in gray and white and fiery red, for as far as the eye can see.

Jan stood on the hill and looked out over this gargantuan tableau. After an additional minute or two, she looked down past her feet to where the cemetery lay. All of these people had consciously committed to making this austere, twisted, weathered land their home, or their forebears had made it for them. But in any case, it had been a decision, not a tradition, at some point.

Who would be a pioneer in a place like this? What was their motivation? They had eventually established a comfortable home here, and Jan now understood better the rewards of the nearby countryside. but before anyone knew about that, what had caused them to put down roots and stay here?

Again, as always, why was Wheeler here? Jan accepted Fred's explanation of the creative potential available to Wheeler, but had he known before he came? And if not, how had his wanderings led to this place? Something still seemed to be missing, but Jan could not pin it down.

She retrieved her camera and removed the red filter to allow enough light for handheld shooting. Moving slowly counter-clockwise, she captured a mosaic of exposures to record the entire scene. Then, after stowing it all again, she made her way back down the mountainside to her car.

INTERLUDE: 1941

Jim was standing hunched over, as he did much of the time at work. However, at the moment, he was concerned with a different sort of assignment.

"Ssshhhh," he said softly. "Hush, now. Daddy will get things taken care of. Maybe not smoothly, but he will do the best he can."

Jim was removing rubber shorts and fumbling with safety pins. Dora was off at one of her bridge nights, and the governess they'd hired was at home with a cold. All of which left him to feed little Clara, change her diapers when necessary, and try to determine what she was demanding when she cried.

"Oh, my gosh, kid!" he said, reaching for a damp washcloth. "Where on earth do you keep all of that? You're not that big yet!"

Pull used diaper down a couple of inches. Wash and dry baby, paying special attention to nooks and crannies, of which the average baby has thousands. Transfer baby to clean diaper. Fold clean diaper temporarily over front of baby's pelvic region—very important!—while gathering supplies. Dispense a dollop or two of baby lotion and coat baby evenly. Double-check clean diaper, making sure diaper is still clean. Add a little talcum—thank you for the reminder, Ogden Nash. Now reinsert safety pins, making sure not to bend any, and triple-check to verify that they stay locked. Finally, reapply rubber shorts and pajamas.

"There!" Jim said with a flourish as he dumped the offending material into an adjacent diaper pail. "All done."

Clara was unimpressed.

"Well, then," Jim said to her, "food is the next guess. Just a moment." He transferred Clara to her crib and stepped to the kitchen, where he had left a bottle of formula warming within a water bath he'd set up in one of Dora's saucepans. He drew out the bottle, dried it carefully with a clean towel, and arm-tested the temperature of the formula. Then he returned to the nursery, which had previously been his home office and would in future be Clara's bedroom.

With Clara snug in the crook of his left arm, Jim sat down in the wooden rocking chair and placed the nipple of the bottle next to Clara's lips. Clara, who by this point had long familiarity with these bottles, obliged. Jim rocked while Clara fed. After a few minutes, the baby set the bottle aside and resumed her crying; Jim picked her up and put her face over his left shoulder. He knew few lullabies, so he hummed "Sophisticated Lady" as he rocked slowly back and forth.

Clara burped softly and relaxed, and by the end of "Mood Indigo" she was asleep. Slowly and carefully, Jim transferred her back into her crib and covered her with her little pink blanket. He turned off the overhead light, leaving the small lamp by the crib on, and quietly withdrew.

In the living room, Jim turned on the radio. While he waited for it to warm up, he picked up the day's newspaper from the coffee table. When the radio finally began to sound, he made sure to turn it down so that Clara wouldn't be disturbed. But as he read the paper, there was nothing to prevent him from being disturbed. Japan was continuing to grab up land in Asia, and making noises as though they remained hungry for more. They were almost as widespread as Hitler now, and of course, Hitler was everywhere. People were becoming nervous and unsteady. The country had spent a long, miserable decade slogging through the aftermath of the stock market collapse, and now it increasingly seemed that sooner or later, war would come. The only real question was when and how.

But Chambers, of course, showed no indecision. Wars meant production, and he meant to own as much of that production as he could. If the depression had never forced its way into the halls of Chambers Industries, the coming conflict was being ushered in as an honored guest.

Jim had recently accompanied Chambers as photographer on a sweep of new facilities he was building in West Coast cities, and he was still awash in the resulting backlog of darkroom work. The man seemed indefatigable, pressing ahead, probing for advantages and vulnerabilities, pounding away at the challenges before him.

The lock on the front door rattled, pulling Jim out of his meditations. The door opened and Dora stepped briskly in.

"Good evening, dear," Jim said.

Dora seemed slightly disoriented. She spun leftward to regard him. "What are you doing here?" she asked in an agitated voice. "Where is Loretta?"

"Loretta is at home with a cold," Jim replied, "and I am here tending Clara, so that with any luck, that cold doesn't reach her.

"That loafer! This the second time in two months she's called in sick. She'd better not do it again, or she'll have more to make her sick. And you have work to finish at the office, too, or we won't be able to keep a governess. And I warn you, that will not make me happy."

As Dora swung her coat onto the rack next to the door, Jim tried to identify the scent it swept toward him. It was strangely complex, but that made sense given where she'd been.

"Well, don't worry, dear," Jim assured his wife. "I do have a lot of developing and printing work to do, but I keep a sharp eye on my pacing. I understand which side my bread is buttered on, believe me. How was bridge?"

"Huh?" Dora took a moment to focus. "Oh, fine. Typical, really. We had a guest player named Mary Ann who kept flubbing her bidding, but otherwise nothing unusual. Why do you ask?"

"No reason, really. Just small talk."

Dora said nothing further, but strode into the bedroom to shed her social outfit and its accompanying straps and harnesses. Immediately afterward, Jim could hear water running in the bathtub. He noticed the tenor of his conversations with his wife to be returning to the pattern of monosyllables and insults that had been the norm throughout much of their marriage. After the brief respite before Clara was born, it did seem as though the walls were going back up.

Jim heard a coughing sound from the nursery, and Clara began to cry. He jumped up and slapped the newspaper back onto the coffee table.

"Hang on, kid!" Jim called. "I'm on my way!"

NINE

"How are things going?" Wheeler asked Jan.

"I think I'm on track, or slightly ahead," Jan said. "It's been going pretty much the way I expected. As I get into the older negatives, your notes aren't quite so automatic, if that makes any sense, because we're using different materials now. So I'm running lots of test strips, and sheets sometimes. For manipulations I try to keep to what your intent was; I follow your diagrams wherever I can, but it seems like the dodging and burning drops off a little differently around the edges."

"Okay, how are we doing on paper?"

"We may be running low on the grade three."

"All right. I'll put in a rush order."

Jan hesitated a moment. "Could I ask your advice on something?"

"Well, if it's about dating, I'm probably not the best guy to ask."

Jan glowered a moment. "Photography," she said. "It's a technical question."

"Oh, those I'm pretty good at," Jim said.

"I tried to do a nighttime shot the other night, with all the tourists blowing through town after sunset. I checked and double-checked my settings, but the prints still look muddy."

"Do you have one of them?"

"Yeah, here's one. And here are the negatives," Jan said, carefully placing a piece of typing paper on Wheeler's desk and then laying down a strip of film on the paper.

"Well, it is muddy, unfortunately. How long of an exposure did you use?

"About two minutes."

Wheeler picked up the film and held it where he could look through it at the curtains on the nearest window. He turned it one way, then the other.

"It looks like you've fallen prey to reciprocity failure, Jan."

"Say what?"

Wheeler looked at her for a moment. "In your classes, I'm guessing you've been shooting under well-controlled conditions? Direct sunlight, studio flash systems, that kind of thing?"

"Usually, yes."

"Have you done many time exposures before?"

"A few," Jan said. "They've been pretty hit and miss."

"Did you borrow one of my meters for this?"

"Yes, I did. Thanks for the offer, by the way."

"Don't mention it. But if you're actually going to figure a long exposure like this, sometimes you have to figure reciprocity failure in."

"Okay, so what is it?"

"In your classes, once they tell you to turn the automatic settings off on your camera, they probably start with the basic exposure formula, right? Intensity times time. So, the less light you have to work with, the more time you have to add.

"*But* ... that formula only works in controlled conditions, because film has molecular limitations when you go outside those conditions. With really small amounts of light, it actually takes longer to respond. So what that means," Wheeler said, spreading his hands to illustrate, "is that you're thinking, 'the less light, the more time,' but your *film* is thinking, 'the less light, the more time, and the more time, the more time.'"

"Ugh," said Jan.

"There's also an adjustment you should make to your development, although with rollfilm you may have to do without that—or fudge in even more time. But don't worry, all this stuff is written up and published, nice and neat. I can lend you the reference sheet I have for Tri-X.

"This is kind of the photographer's way of saying that two things that are equal to the same thing aren't equal to one another." Wheeler gave one of his grins. "By the way, have you had any more trouble with the metal reels?"

"No, it's fine. I sacrificed a roll of film and practiced until I had the feel of it and could do it blind."

"Good, good. Listen, there are two things. One of them is that I'll need the darkroom this evening so that I can work on Carol's portraits. They still need to be kept confidential until she has had the opportunity to review them."

"Okay, no problem. I can go say hi to Jenny, or maybe see if Carol is off work."

"The other thing is that people are starting to track me down, and someone is showing up here in a few minutes to do an interview. God help me." Wheeler shook his head. "Anyway, you're welcome to sit on the sidelines if you're curious."

A few minutes later, two people arrived in Wheeler's office: a reporter and the photographer who came to illustrate her story. Wheeler greeted them politely, and then threw the entire session off track by poking, prodding, and cooing over the photographer's camera and flash setup.

"If we could begin with the questions, Mr. Wheeler?" the reporter asked with some added force in her voice."

"Oh, of course, of course," Wheeler said. "Please forgive me. A morbid curiosity about technology comes with the territory, I'm afraid. I think that at least so far, photography is unique that way. I've never heard of one painter saying to another one, 'Oh, I have to look at that brush of yours.' Or a sculptor saying, 'Hey, nice chisel. What's its top speed?'"

Her photographer lowered his camera for a moment and flashed a thumbs-up sign at Wheeler, who nodded back. The photographer returned to his previous pattern of squeezing off a shot when Wheeler showed an interesting expression or gesture.

"By the way," Wheeler continued, "when we're done here, there's something I'd like to show you guys that may be useful for the article. Once the word gets out, people will probably be building some of their own, and if you can mention that I did it first, I'd like that. Sorry again. First question?"

Many of the reporter's questions were similar to the ones the students in Laramie had asked when Jan had arrived at the beginning of the summer, but Jan heard a few bits of additional information. Wheeler had spent a few years in residence for six-month stretches with a company in Casper, which was presumably where the post office box there had come into the story. From his experience in Casper, he said, he had come to understand that there were places in the north and west of the state, but not too close to Yellowstone, where he could survive on his income and continue his craft.

"Creating pieces like that exquisite thing behind you?"

"Thank you," Wheeler said. "That's about ten or fifteen years old. Devil's Tower, obviously. But no aliens. We didn't know about the aliens back then."

"Do you have any newer work?"

"Of course. Much of it has never been seen, and some of it has never been printed. Jan over there —" he motioned to the side of the room where she was sitting, and she smiled and nodded, "— has been out here for about a month now, helping me prepare them for the exhibit I'm going to be giving down at the university in Laramie.

"It'll be running between the first week of August and the last week of October, and it's a career retrospective," Wheeler continued, then paused. "Actually, let's say 'works to date.' 'Career retrospective' sounds like I'm about to die, which I hope isn't true. But some of my older stuff will be there, and some of the work I've been stockpiling more recently. There will also be a few experiments, like some dye-transfer color prints I've been working on."

"It sounds great," the reporter said. "But why haven't you printed or shown your more recent work until now?"

"Well, as I say, I went through some pretty tough times for a while. By the time they steadied out, the art had changed. What I knew how to do was pretty old-school, large-format black-and-white mostly. The photography that was selling best was smaller formats, and almost all of it was high-saturation color reversal film, and I was still playing catch-up.

"When interest in the older black-and-white forms started to pick back up, I was happy to hear about it, but I hadn't heard that interest had spread beyond a few big names—Adams, Weston, Minor White, a few others. I didn't know that I was on anyone's radar at all, until Jan showed up one day last summer and told me so."

"One of my college instructors had mentioned it to me," Jan added.

"All right," said the reporter. "Would you mind a couple of philosophical questions?"

"Well, no one is going to mistake me for a philosopher," Wheeler said, "but go ahead."

The photographer set himself for a reaction shot as the reporter adjusted herself slightly in her chair. "Can the camera lie?" she asked.

For a fraction of a second, to Jan's surprise, Wheeler looked shocked and hurt, as though the reporter had just kicked him in the shin. He recovered quickly and spent a few seconds in thought. "Can a sock puppet lie?" he asked the reporter.

"What do you mean?" she responded.

Wheeler was back to the sphinx impersonation he had adopted during Jan's first visit. He repeated, "Can a sock puppet lie?"

The reporter was becoming irritated. "I do not understand what you are driving at," she said with a slight growl.

"Guy with a sock puppet. He's moving his hand and making the puppet say things. Is the puppet telling the truth?"

"The man operating the puppet is actually deciding what to say."

Wheeler sat back and folded his arms. "Exactly!" he said. "A person with a camera could show up, right here in Thermopolis, and could end up taking a roll of film of a little tourist town … or of a place unlike any other place in the country. I suspect that by now, Jan has photos of both." Jan nodded. "Truth and lies are values that people assign. A camera records its owner's interpretation." The photographer looked up and nodded as well.

"And that may change, too," Wheeler continued. "I understand that when he died, Adams was messing around with computers, in the belief that they may become involved in photography. At that point, in addition to not being true or false, photographs may not even be factual. We won't know until we see what happens."

"All right, one more," the reporter said as she tried to adjust herself back to a brighter demeanor. "You're in the middle of a sudden return of interest in a career that you've pursued for decades in the face of stiff challenges. What would you say to young people about the importance of following their passion?"

Once again, there was a fleeting expression on Wheeler's face. This time it just looked tired and painful. Again, he recovered quickly and spoke.

"I'd tell 'em not to do it," he said.

"Well, that's disappointing," the reporter persisted. "Why do you say that?"

"I'm not saying they should abandon their dreams or their goals," Wheeler continued. "But 'follow your passion' is the wrong way of putting it. Passion is a terrible guide. It's like your own personal Lansford Hastings."

"Who?"

"Sorry. That was a bad reference. But I would tell the kids that they have to be aware of the risks and the tradeoffs. Sometimes, serving the things that give your life most of its meaning require work and sacrifice—and I mean *hard* work, and *painful* sacrifices. That's what happened to me.

"The alternative is to remove those meanings from your life and just do what's most comfortable, and some people go that way. Everyone makes their own decision. The problem with 'follow your passion' is that the saying implies that it's easy. It's not. But a lot of the time, it's worth the trouble." Wheeler blinked. "I guess if you wanted something really heavy and depressing, that'll do it. Sorry about that."

"We'll see what we can do with it," the reporter said. "Thanks for your time."

"Oh, wait!" Wheeler said. "There was the thing I wanted to show you and your young man, remember?" He stood up and grabbed the greenhouse key from his desk drawer. "Do you have an extra minute?"

"Yeah, I think so."

"Okay, step this way, then."

Wheeler unlocked the greenhouse and escorted the two visitors into his solar studio. The photographer looked around himself, then up, then around again. Then he snorted once, and finally started to laugh. Within ten seconds he was laughing loudly.

"Holy *shit!*" he said.

"Not bad, huh?" Wheeler responded.

"These canopies ... do they retract?"

"Yes, they do. Separately or together, as you need."

"The side screens move?"

"Of course."

"And you use these reflectors to fine-tune the light in the space."

"Yes," Wheeler said. "Of course, you could use commercial light-shapers too. I was trying to save some money."

"It's a bit warm in here, isn't it?" the reporter asked.

"Oh, there's actually ventilation," Wheeler answered. "We're getting into the season where the ventilation isn't always enough, but it works well most of the year."

The photographer looked around himself again and chuckled. "Well," he said, "when I get home, I'm building one in my own backyard. But I'll give you full credit, don't worry."

INTERLUDE: LATE 1942

"Win her heart."

Those were the words people used in Jim's childhood. They would meet at weddings and give best wishes to the bride and congratulations to the groom, because she was embarking on a risky new chapter in her life, but he had won her heart. And then they would ask him how he'd done it.

The answer usually involved harrying the poor young woman day and night, for weeks and months and years on end, until she gave up and agreed to his third or fifth or fifteenth marriage proposal. And when she said yes, that was how he knew he'd succeeded.

And so, when he reached his sixteenth year, that was what Jim figured he needed to do.

A year later, when he first encountered Dora MacKinnon, she had just turned sixteen herself, but she already shone and sparkled like no one else in the neighborhood where the two of them lived. Young men vied relentlessly for her attention, and she would humor them and then dismiss them, one at a time and sometimes more than once. She enjoyed being at the center of things and the power that came with her position at the focus of it all.

At some point, Jim had seen her in the midst of her retinue and decided that he would be the one to do it. He would win her heart.

And at that point, a strange dance began. Jim would pursue Dora directly and she would put him off, and he would pursue her again and she would put him off again, and he would pursue her yet a third time and she would accompany him for a week or two before dropping him again. And then he would make sure he saw her in the company of another young woman, which made Dora insanely jealous, and then she would do something to ensure that he returned.

In time, many of the young men grew weary and disenchanted, and when they left, Dora was unable to draw them back into the game. And so the day came when her suitors consisted of one young, somewhat overly romantic photographer's assistant, one farmer's son, and one mechanic. And when the photographer's assistant asked for her hand in marriage, she relented.

Jim was happy. He had succeeded. By the rules of the game, he had won her heart.

But there were two problems.

First, the rules of the game didn't really pay much attention to the contents of the young lady's heart, because they couldn't. It was assumed that she would never commit to something that large without full assent of her mind, heart, and soul. But often, the young lady's decision was built on facts, figures, and probabilities instead of any nobler considerations.

Second, the rules paid no attention at all to the young gentleman's heart. They cared not at all whether he felt any genuine love for her, or whether he was only attempting to claim her for the sake of the prize she represented, or even—as often occurred—whether he was actually bidding not for her heart, but for other features closer to her center of gravity.

Jim and Dora had had a brief, sunny time together after the wedding. For the first couple of years, he would hurry home when work ended for the day and they would laugh and snuggle together, entertaining one another with the private references and silly jokes that all newlyweds share. But the jokes and the embraces got rarer and rarer over the following months, and the sunlight gradually faded. Eventually, they had dwindled to a pair of imperfectly matched roommates.

Jim sat at the desk in his office and pondered all of this. He had just finished one of his regular shoots with Zoë, and they had followed their usual routine. She went into the dressing room and put on whatever was going into the next newspaper brochure, and while Jim took his meter readings and twiddled the rings and dials on his camera, she would ask him how his life was going and pepper him with affectionate mock insults. And while they were doing this, questions were forming in the back of Jim's mind.

All the while he had been growing up, and coming of age, and competing for Dora's ever-contested heart, he had played the game by the rules. And so, he had never examined how he himself felt about it. He understood that his role now was to build a stable existence for Dora, and he was committed to fulfilling that role. But it had never occurred to him that the tables might turn, and someone might unexpectedly win *his* heart.

And that afternoon, after changing and reporting back for a new set of shots, Zoë had asked Jim to check the makeup around her eyes. He had leaned over and looked directly into them. And he had become aware of something—not a sudden realization, but a final recognition of something that had been waiting there for a while.

Zoë Quinlan had truly won his heart.

He couldn't identify exactly when this had happened, but it definitely had. He was caught as though chained to two rocks shifting in opposite directions. On one side was his commitment to fulfilling his duty to his wife and keeping his word. On the other was the fire he felt in his soul whenever Zoë spoke to him.

And in that moment, when he had looked so deeply into those beautiful, dark eyes, he thought he saw that same fire reflected back. Just for a tiny instant, the pain and longing in his own heart was also graven in Zoë's magnificent eyes.

Soon enough, she had gotten back into her own outfit, and he had helped her into her coat and watched her click her way down the sidewalk as always. But as he watched her go, shoulders back and head high, he found himself wondering what he could do. Objectively, of course, he could do nothing at all. He could not destroy his own marriage, and he certainly couldn't create the sort of damage that an affair would cause in Zoë's life.

In any case, he might be deluding himself. He might have imagined what he saw, or created it out of his own wants. If he ever asked her, he might lose a valuable friend and ally without good reason.

But as he sat at his desk that night, attempting to catch up on business, Jim was consumed by two questions:

First, when he was nineteen, why hadn't he examined his own heart?

And second, by all the gods in all the heavens in all the universe, why hadn't he met Zoë first?

TEN

Jan stood in the dingy yellow light and musty, vaguely sulfurous air, evaluating the sheet of paper before her. The edges of the door frame were a little sloppy yet, so she wadded up the paper and threw it in the discard bin. Then she went to the hand-washing sink, washed and dried her hands thoroughly, and turned back toward the dry side of the darkroom.

The negative was still in the contact frame, underneath a sheet of glass that she painstakingly wiped clean and swept free of dust each morning; the tiniest speck would become a white spot that she or Wheeler would need to touch out later, at which point any twitch might send her back here. She removed a new sheet of paper from the appropriate lightsafe box, opened the frame, and positioned the paper under the negative. Then, after closing the frame again, she brushed the top surface of the glass again and went over it with a bulb blower, just to make absolutely sure.

Jan slid the frame under the enlarger next to her, adjusted the timer, and pressed the power button immediately. Even after the past few weeks, it still seemed a little odd to Jan that she never actually put the film in the enlarger and never did any focusing. But Wheeler had gone over the whole practice and its long history with her.

"I've had this since I was a young man," he had said, motioning toward the big view camera in his studio, "and I've managed to hang on to it ever since. I've coughed up the money necessary to keep the shutter in tune and the bellows tight, even if it wasn't easy, because once the prices started going up, there was no way I could have replaced it. But there were three big reasons for that.

"First, such a huge negative grabs tons of detail—if you've got a decent lens, at least.

"Second, if you're making eight-by-ten prints, you can skip the enlarger, except as a source of light. All of the messing around with enlarger focusing, considerations about what printing aperture to use, any irregularities in the enlarging lens, all of that just drops away.

"And last, when you enlarge a piece of film, you also dilute it. It thins out a bit. You can compensate for that, but doing it this way, most of the richness in the original transfers right onto the paper."

When the timer clicked off, Jan made a second setting. She reached for the box of manipulation tools and grabbed a piece of posterboard with a small, round hole in it. Holding the board a short distance over the contact frame, she pressed the timer button again and moved the board in small, careful circles.

After repeating this process one more time with a different piece of posterboard, Jan retrieved the printing paper from the frame. She pivoted a half turn to the side of the room where the developing trays were and submerged the paper. She began to rock the tray, and every so often she reached in with tongs and turned the paper over.

When the image on the paper had solidified, she moved it through the remaining baths and rinsed it for a few minutes in a square tank with running water flowing through it. She took a critical look at the image as it floated just below the water's surface.

The photograph was unusual among Wheeler's more typical work. He had taken it in his youth somewhere along the Big Sur coast, which was not one of his customary haunts. Also, it lacked the defocused backgrounds of most of his later images. But like almost all of his work, it was dramatic and compelling, even though the subject—two cypress trees on a jagged boulder—was extremely simple.

The two trees gripped the stone securely with scarred, weathered, twisted roots. Their bowed trunks leaned westward, holding out spindly branches in opposition to the winds and storms that had originally bent them. Combined with the slant of evening light that animated the ends of the branches, Wheeler's composition lent the trees an aspect of powerless, sullen, spiteful defiance against a hostile, oppressive god.

The tonal aspects of the image, and all the objects in it, looked appropriate to Jan. There weren't any light or dark splotches to indicate that her adjustments had landed in the wrong place. So when the print was done with its first rinse, she carefully transferred it to a paper washer through which a trickle of water ran steadily. She would need to finish rinsing it, allow it to dry, and then evaluate it again; if it still met her requirements by then, she would take it to Wheeler for his final critique, and with luck, his approval.

Because of the way in which Wheeler had eased Jan into her work, starting with the newest and easiest negatives and working backward, she considered herself the beneficiary of an intensive reverse review of his career. If Fred Lopez dared to question her about Wheeler now, by God, she could bore him all the way into a coma, starting with how Wheeler mimicked Stieglitz and Weston in his youth and elaborating on how his visual identity emerged over the decades. In that hypothetical situation, she would be sure to remind Fred of Wheeler's tendency to emphasize traces of humanity in his work and provide multiple examples. She would also be sure to tell him that in recent years, Wheeler had visited most of the sites he had pointed out around

Thermopolis on the map in the university library. Of course, with Fred asking for updates by mail every couple of weeks, it was equally likely that none of this information was news to him.

With her hands thoroughly washed and dried, Jan pivoted back to the enlarger. With extreme care, she removed the negative from the contact frame and returned it to the appropriate folder in the storage binder. She retrieved the next negative in the sequence that Wheeler had given her, installed it into the frame, then added a strip of printing paper and began her exposure tests.

Among the example prints that Wheeler kept in the binders, the image that she was now printing was one of her favorites. As she locked in the exposure and did her first full test print, a new copy emerged.

On a featureless plain under a measureless formation of small cumulus clouds, half of a frame house stood. Some human intrusion or force of nature had ripped away the other half, leaving the kitchen and the main bedroom open to the elements, and Wheeler had arranged the image to draw the viewer's eye to the bedroom. Oddly, even though the room was no longer enclosed or complete, the woodwork and wallpaper on the remaining walls seemed intact, and a dirty fringe of thin curtain remained over the window on the back wall. Somehow, when Jan looked at the photograph, she felt as though she was peering without permission into the *sanctum sanctorum* of someone's daily life, and words formed unbidden in the space within her mind:

This was the core of a couple's existence once. They dressed here, undressed here, fought here, consoled one another here, made love here, shivered with fever here. They lived here and they may have died here. But they are gone, and everything they cared for has been scattered afar.

Jan reached into the box of manipulation tools and withdrew a small length of fine wire with tiny cotton balls of two different sizes on either end. She had created this dodging tool herself when she felt the need for something finer and more precise than the tools Wheeler owned. When she had shown it to him, his only reaction had been, "Well, go ahead and use it. If it works, I'll use it too."

She pressed the timer button and moved her homemade dodging tool over the bedroom, digging excess shadow out of the corners of the room while at the same time shifting her hand to prevent the skewer from leaving a mark. The exposure ended and she set up for another.

After a few hours of this, the half-house had joined the cypress trees in the print washer. Jan washed and dried her hands again and returned the negative to the binder. She suppressed a small wave of apprehension on noticing that the next image on Wheeler's list was none other than *Barnyard, Modesto, 1945,* the original image that had caught Fred's attention. That negative was in a different binder, so she shut the binder she had with her and climbed the stairs toward the storage closet that contained Wheeler's master files.

In the closet, Jan slid the binder back into the space from which she had removed it and went in search of the one she needed next. Her eyes traced their way along the topmost shelf, then the second one, until she found the object of her search. She slid it out and set it aside, but then she stopped.

Next to the space she had just opened up sat a binder that looked different from the others. The patent leather on its covers was dark brown instead of black, and it bore the marks of age and long use. Jan carefully slid it out, placed it on an adjacent counter, and opened the front cover. She stopped in surprise.

There in front of her, sharp and rich in nuanced detail, was a portrait of her grandmother. But this was not the bowed, angry, white-haired woman she remembered from her childhood. The woman in the photograph was tall, slender, and shockingly beautiful, with her blonde hair in pincurls and a vaguely haughty expression on her smooth, unblemished face. One of her eyebrows arched slightly, as though she was preparing to challenge the photographer over something.

Several additional portraits and family snapshots followed; Jan allowed herself a smile at how different San Francisco had looked when the snapshots were taken. Most of these had dates penciled on their backs, and almost all of them had been taken between 1937 and 1939.

Next, Jan found a portrait of her mother—in a crib, in 1941. In subsequent portraits, the tiny infant grew into an inquisitive toddler. Little Clara's straight dark hair formed an attractive contrast to her mother's light curls when the two of them appeared together, but none of these photographs was dated later than 1946.

Jan flipped another divider to the side, and had to shake her head to clear it. The pit of her stomach felt as though she had been punched there, and her heartbeat sped up and intensified.

In front of her was another picture of her grandmother. She stood inside the doorway of a building with her arms around a dark-haired man in an expensive-looking business suit. Unlike Wheeler's typical polished work, this photograph was splotchy and gritty from large film grains.

Jan flipped through the additional pictures in this section of the binder. They showed the unknown man grasping at her grandmother and kissing her. Jan felt slightly ill.

On the back of the last photograph in the sequence a penciled note read as follows:

D. MacK. W. / F. Chambers. VII/1943.

Jan shook her head again. *Frank Chambers?*

Immediately behind her, Wheeler cleared his throat. Startled, she jumped a foot back.

"You weren't supposed to see that," he said.

"I am so sorry," she answered, her words rushed. "I came up to get my next negative, and this binder was right next to it. It was an accident."

"I understand," Wheeler said. "When I said you weren't supposed to see that, that's exactly what I meant. There was a group of binders that I pulled out and stored elsewhere for your visit, because I wanted to keep them confidential—mostly client negatives, actually. But this one was supposed to go with them. I must have missed it." He motioned into his office. "Come sit down for a second."

Jan sat in one of the client chairs next to Wheeler's desk, head bent over. The pain in the pit of her stomach had not subsided. Wheeler sat in his own chair, watching her closely. "Are you all right?" he asked.

"I'll be okay in a minute," Jan answered him.

"All right," said Wheeler. He continued watching Jan until her breathing had calmed a little. Eventually, he spoke again.

"Is there anything you need to know?" he asked.

Jan had many questions, but many of them were too intrusive for her to ask at the moment. "When did you and Grandma get divorced?" she finally asked.

"1946," Wheeler said.

"Were those pictures part of the divorce trial?"

"No. There was no trial."

"Why not?"

Wheeler's gaze dropped for a moment, and he hesitated before he spoke. "Innocent people would have been hurt," he said.

"Grandma was involved with Frank Chambers?" Jan asked.

"Yes."

"Is that why innocent people would have been hurt?"

"Partly," Wheeler said. "There were other things."

"But I was always told that you were the one who …"

"I was. Remember what I told that fellow in Laramie the night you showed up?" Wheeler shook his head slightly. "At the time of the divorce, I was guilty as charged, and I had to face the consequences."

The pain in the pit of Jan's stomach had begun to subside, but was now strengthening again. "But that was three years later," she protested.

Wheeler gave small, mirthless laugh. "Look, I don't think I should go into those details," he said. "It was a mess, and I played a part in it. That's all you need to know for now.

"If you have more work to do, you can go ahead and do it. I'm going to head out for a couple of hours, so if you need to leave before I get back, please lock the door on your way out."

Jan went over her remaining work and her schedule quickly, and decided it was better not to attempt any more printing work that day. Her stomach had settled down a bit, but her mind was still too unsteady. As far back as she could remember, she had been told that her grandfather had betrayed the family through his infidelity. But now it looked as though he was only responding to a betrayal of his own.

And why would her grandmother do such a thing? In Jan's own experience, Chambers was an old man and a target for anti-corporate protests on campus. In his youth—as handsome, wealthy, and strong-willed as he had apparently been—was he just too compelling to pass up? Or had something else been involved?

INTERLUDE: 1943

Jim let Zoë in and helped her out of her coat as usual. "How are things?" she asked him.

"Depends on the things," he replied.

"Well, that's a nice, evasive response," Zoë said. "What do we have today?"

"A few hand things," Jim said.

"Are these the good kind of things?" she asked. "Helpful or unhelpful?"

"Helpful, if they make us a few bucks. Right?"

"Always the pragmatist." Zoë peered into Jim's office for a moment as they walked by. "Speaking of things, you have an unusual thing on your desk."

"Oh, yeah." Jim's voice perked up a bit. "Salesman came by yesterday, asked me to keep it for a few days to check it out. He said I could keep it for a two-week trial if I wanted."

"So what is it?"

"Leica," Jim said, directing her into the office. "Have you seen one?"

"No."

"It's a miniature camera that runs on rolls of movie film." He carefully handed it to her. "Did you want to look at it?" he asked. "Be careful. It's built like a fine watch, so I have to assume it breaks like one too."

"Is it loaded?" Zoë asked.

"No, not yet," Jim answered. "I hadn't decided whether I wanted to take the fellow up on his two-week offer."

Zoë looked through the rangefinder, made adjustments, clicked the shutter and tested some of the other controls. "Well, it's certainly cute," she said.

"It might also come in handy if you didn't want to call attention to yourself," Jim added. "Problem is, I don't do any sort of work where I have to go incognito."

"Well, maybe you should think of something, while it's on loan. I don't know." Zoë put the little camera back down on the desk.

The afternoon's session didn't last very long, and Jim saw Zoë to the door.

"Hey, what's that?" she asked, bending over and picking up a business card that rested next to the base of the door. She picked it up and read it aloud.

"'The horns are on'?" Zoë twisted up her face in confusion. "What does that even mean?"

"I have no idea," Jim said. "I don't even drive to work, so it doesn't have to do with my car. Whose business card is it?"

Zoë turned it over and immediately looked even more confused. "It's yours."

"Mine?" Jim was thinking quickly, but not reaching any useful conclusions. "Who would take one of my cards and return it to me with a secret message about horns?" Suddenly, the back corner of his mind's attic yielded forth a long-disused piece of information and his face fell in shock. "Oh ..."

"What is it?" Zoë asked. "Did you figure it out?"

Jim nodded. "It's an expression from hundreds of years ago. Shakespeare's time, maybe earlier. Back then, when your wife was cheating on you, they said that she'd put horns on you. But why use my card?"

Zoë had a quick explanation. "It's not *his* card."

"Right."

"It also probably means that whoever left this either does business with you directly, or the culprit does." Zoë thought for a moment. "Or your wife may have been unfaithful more than once. The guy she dumped may have gotten one of your cards from her, and he's returning it to you now in an act of revenge." She looked at the expression on Jim's face. "Sorry."

"It's okay," Jim said. "This could explain a lot, but it's also a lot to take in."

Zoë leaned over and looked at him more closely, her eyes showing her concern. "Are you all right?"

"I think so." Jim straightened up and put his shoulders back. "This could still be a prank, and we don't know where it came from in any case. But I'll need to make sure." He looked back toward his office. "I think maybe I'll take that trial."

Jim was not a drinker. He did not drink. He was nursing a bottle of cheap Scotch at the moment, but he wasn't a drinker. Not as a rule.

Two weeks had passed since he had received the enigmatic card, and he was sitting in his office. In front of him, on his desk, were prints of the photographs he had taken of Dora with Frank Chambers. He felt like he needed another drink. But he wasn't a drinker, as a rule. He took another drink.

He had tried so hard. All the ice-cold evenings, the offhanded insults, the exaggerated flirting between Dora and Chambers. The goddamned "bridge" nights. He'd always hoped he could save the marriage somehow. He wasn't a drinker. All the time gone, all gone.

Zoë had been at the studio earlier, modeling a few jackets for the Capwell's account. She'd seen the photo on his desk.

"Oh, my God," she'd said, one hand over her mouth. "That's Dora, isn't it?"

"Yeah."

"With *Frank Chambers?*"

Jim nodded.

"Jim, I warned you that he was trouble. But I didn't expect this. My God, she's carrying on with *him?*" Zoë made a face. "Ugh. So when was this?"

"Last weekend," Jim had said. "Dora told me she was out of town visiting her sister. Then I saw her with Chambers up near Union Square. I don't think they saw me."

He was not a drinker. He was not.

"Dear God," Zoë had said. "You poor guy. What are you going to do, get a lawyer?"

"I don't know."

Zoë had done an enormous double take. "You *don't know?* You're kidding, right?"

"If I divorced her over this and used the photo as evidence, it could ruin her."

"But, if you don't, it could ruin *you*. Jim, you have a right to a happy life. Especially with all of this going on." She had waved toward the photograph.

"I don't really know how I deal with this yet. It's too big."

Zoë had leaned over to look at him face-to-face. "Listen," she said intently, "if I can help you in any way, you just let me know. All right?"

"All right."

And then he had let her out the front door of his business as usual and she had clicked her way down the street. Jim had stopped watching her walk away several months earlier; her swiveling gait, which he had originally found amusing, was now painful to watch.

He was not a drinker. Not normally.

Jim sat and thought about Zoë. She had been a constant in his life throughout the past four years of uncertainty and pain. And as the years had gone on, a fire had begun to grow inside him when he thought of her. It wasn't right, and he needed to get rid of it somehow.

She had been helpful and supportive without fail. Also smart-assed, but always helpful and supportive. He couldn't lose that, mustn't do anything to mess it up.

"If I can help you in any way ..."

He was not an adulterer.

It was seven in the evening, with rain coming down again, when Jim staggered up to the address on Zoë's business card. He rang the doorbell and pounded on the door. "Zoë!" he called. "Zoë!"

Footsteps hastened to the door, and the lock disengaged. "Jim?" Zoë asked. "What is it? What's wrong?" She was standing before him in a bathrobe and fuzzy slippers, with a towel wrapped around her head. "Dear God, what happened to you?"

"I need you."

"I beg your pardon?"

"I love you, and I need your help. My wife's sleeping around on me and I'm alone."

He staggered toward her and collapsed against the wrought-iron railing.

Zoë studied the pathetic figure in front of her for a minute or two.

"Jim," she said at last, "you're drunk. Go home."

"But I need you …"

"I said go home," Zoë repeated firmly. "I want you to think about all of this when you've sobered up. Then you can come back and tell me anything that you really mean. Deal?"

"But right now I need …"

"Jim," Zoë repeated quietly, "go home. I will see you in a day or two."

As Zoë watched Jim stumble away, she brushed a tear away from her cheek. For many months now, she had continued chattering and needling him when she worked with him, burying deep the longing in her spirit. And now, she had heard Jim say the words she long dreamed of hearing from him, but she had no way of knowing whether they were true.

Jim awoke the next morning with a combination of seasickness and what felt like a mass of burning cotton in his head. He was most definitely not a drinker, as a rule.

As he showered, brushed his teeth, and shaved, vague memories of his visit to Zoë's apartment floated to the surface of his mind. He grimaced with the recollections and his physical pain. He would need to talk to Zoë somehow and apologize.

He stopped in the living room on his way to work. Dora was sitting on her favorite chaise, eating a piece of buttered toast and reading the newspaper.

"Good morning, dear," he said. Dora muttered something in response without looking up.

"Sorry, what was that, dear?"

"You didn't come home drunk last night, did you?"

"I did have a couple of drinks. Hopefully it didn't cause too much trouble."

"Why, no." Dora's eyes were still on her reading. "I just figured a herd of buffalo had managed to break into our bedroom in the middle of the night. No big deal. Honestly, if you're going to let yourself go like that, the sofa might be a better place to sober up."

"Good to see you, too, dear." Jim left for work.

After he locked up in the evening, he walked once again to Zoë's apartment. This time, when she opened the door, she was dressed in a sensible-looking blouse and slacks.

"Hello, Jim," she said. "How are you? Better, I hope?"

"Yes, better," he replied. "May I step in for a moment?"

"All right."

Zoë's living room was small but neat, with a tidy little sofa, a rocking chair, a coat rack nearly fully laden with her jackets and hats, and a few other items. Jim looked around for a moment, then looked back at her.

"I came to apologize," he said.

“Absolutely not necessary,” Zoë responded. “Look, things are tough for you right now, and I know that. But if you’re gonna drink like that, maybe you should do it at home or something, huh?”

“Well, I don’t think I’ll be doing any more of it,” Jim said with one of his little grins, while holding his hands to his temples to illustrate how he’d awakened. “I’ll have to come up with some other way of dealing with everything. I don’t know what I was thinking.”

“Maybe you weren’t. I know the feeling.” Zoë smiled up at him. “Just remember what I said yesterday afternoon. I’ll be happy to help, if I can.”

At her words, a shadow of pain seemed to brush Jim’s face. “What is it?” Zoë asked him. “Are you all right?”

“Yeah, fine, I guess,” Jim said. “It’s just that things are so bad, and you’ve been so kind, and I …”

Zoë leaned forward a bit. “And you what?”

Jim said nothing for about five seconds. Then, suddenly, he leaned down and placed a kiss on Zoë’s full lips. It wasn’t a big kiss, and it didn’t last very long. Afterward, the two of them looked each other in the face and blinked in surprise.

Suddenly, they both lunged. There was a melée of lips, hands, hair, tongues, teeth, and a foot or two. Something crashed to the floor nearby. The few attempts at speech were muffled nearly out of existence.

And then, as suddenly as it had begun, they broke apart again and it was over.

The two of them staggered away, their breathing ragged, their faces twisted in pain and adoration and regret.

To Jim, Zoë appeared to glow, and there seemed to be too much of her perfume in the air. Her expression was the same as his, but he couldn't tell whether she was as ashamed as he was or simply hurt. He looked away.

"I've knocked your coat rack over," he muttered. "Let me clean that up ..."

Zoë grasped his wrist and gently directed him back to face her. "No ..." she said softly, "... no."

"I should go."

Zoë looked confused, but quietly repeated, "No."

Every cell in Jim's body was screaming at him. It was the same fire that had tormented him over the past several weeks every time he thought of her, but it burned much hotter now. Against this background, his mind was tearing itself to pieces. He had hurt Zoë, his friend, his love, his friend. He must apologize and leave, and he must lie with her forever and ever. He could not do this. He was married. He had a wife. But was Dora his wife now? The wheel spun faster, and faster, and faster, and he could not stop it.

He looked imploringly at Zoë, and in a ragged voice, he asked, "What ... do I do?"

And something in Zoë's spirit locked into place. She closed her mouth firmly, set her face into a determined expression, and stepped back in front of Jim. Looking squarely into his eyes, she spoke in a low, level voice that was almost a whisper.

"What you need to do," she said. "You do what you need to do. I'm right here with you."

Two hours later, Zoë sat quietly in her bed. Jim had fallen asleep, and she watched him for a long while, twirling a few strands of hair absentmindedly around her finger.

Eventually she pushed him gently. "Hey," she said.

Jim's eyes opened. He looked around, disoriented. Then, remembering where he was and why, he sat up with a start.

"Zoë, I'm so sorry," he said.

She leaned over, brushed her hair out of her face, and kissed him on the forehead. "Don't you dare," she told him. "Don't you even dare."

"But I ..."

Zoë placed a finger over his lips. "My decision was my own," she said. "I made it myself. And I'm *not* sorry."

"Why, though?"

"I don't know if I can explain that," Zoë said. "Somehow, all of the fears and doubts and hurts just went away, and there were only two things I knew to be true."

"What were those?" Jim asked.

"I loved you, and you were in pain."

She kissed him, slowly and deliberately.

"And now we need to figure out what we do about this situation of ours," she continued. "Where do we go from here?"

"I don't want to bring it to an end," Jim said. "I know that much."

"I don't either." Zoë was standing up, wrapping herself in her bathrobe, and gathering Jim's clothing. "But for right now, we need to get you home in time to avoid attracting attention. You don't want to end up looking like the bad guy when your wife and Frank Chambers are the real villains."

ELEVEN

The midsummer morning sun streamed into Wheeler's office, disrupting the normally muted lighting there. Jan sat in one of the incoming beams and let the warmth loosen the muscles between her shoulder blades, reversing the effects of several consecutive days in the darkroom.

Wheeler's voice resounded from the direction of the kitchen. "Do you see them yet, Jan?"

"Not yet."

"They should have been here by now. If they don't show up in ten minutes or so, I'll call Kate and see if she's seen them."

But within another four minutes, Jan could hear voices outside the door.

"One thing I've always wondered, Kate. How on earth do you keep your face looking so good?"

Jan heard Kate's steady voice in response. "For my age, you mean."

"I didn't mean it that way ..."

"It's all right. No one ever does." Kate paused. "But if you want to know, there are two things. One, wear sun hats. Two, don't smoke." There was another pause. "When I was young, I made the decision never to smoke after I looked around at the older women I knew who had smoked. They all looked like goddamned chimpanzees."

Outside the house, three female voices broke into laughter.

Jan unlocked the front door and let them all in. First came Kate, nodding curtly at her. Second came Michaela, with a shy, little "Hi." And finally, Carol Bradford entered the room.

"Hello, Jan!" she said. "It's good to see you!"

"Likewise, Carol. How are the wedding plans going?"

Carol's smile fell and she raised imploring hands toward heaven. "Insane!" she said. "All the little details are piling up, I have drama breaking out between the bridesmaids—but not the maid of honor, thank you, Michaela!—and the mothers of the happy couple have gone completely psychotic." She suddenly shot an embarrassed glance at Jan. "Sorry," she said. "I didn't mean to unload like that."

Jan laughed. "I asked the question. But come in. Jim's waiting with the proofs."

Wheeler greeted the visitors and motioned them to his desk. "Jan," he said, "I'm going to have to ask you to step away, please. These will still be confidential until the work is finished. You can either sit to one side, or you can step out. It's up to you." Jan took a seat in a far corner of the room.

"Okay," said Wheeler, "I have proofs here of several of our takes. You may remember that I tried a couple of different cameras and a few different kinds of film, so we'll start with the six-by-seven shots."

He opened the binder and placed it in front of Carol. In looking over the portrait that had been placed in front of her, Carol seemed disoriented.

"What's wrong?" Michaela asked.

Carol hesitated. "That's not me," she said.

"Well, it sure looks like you to me," Michaela said. For the first time in months, Jan saw a smile form on Kate's face—not large, and slightly wistful, but definite.

Wheeler said, "If I were to counterfeit a photograph like this, I'd have to find a successful way of duplicating that little tattoo of yours." Carol blushed.

"But these are … *beautiful,*" she said.

"There's an old saying," Wheeler responded quietly. "'You can't put in what God left out.'"

"They're amazing," Carol responded. "These will work perfectly."

"Okay, here are a few more," Wheeler continued as he turned the page. "Personally, I liked the first two, but you may or may not agree."

"No, I think you're right," Carol said. "If we hadn't seen those, I would have been happy with these, but those two are the best so far."

"All right, then," Wheeler said. "When we did the shoot, you may remember that I asked your permission to bring out my old view camera and try it as well. I shot those takes with black-and-white sheets. Remember?"

Carol nodded. "Well," Wheeler said, "here is the best result from that part of the shoot." He slowly turned a divider over within the binder and slid it toward Carol.

Carol looked left, and then right, over the image before her. She leaned over and craned her neck in a couple of directions, looking intently. Finally, she put a hand over her mouth as a tear formed in one eye. She wiped it away, sat back, and looked at Wheeler.

"Those rumors are true, aren't they?" she asked. "You *are* an artist, aren't you?"

"For work like this, I try to be one," Wheeler told her. "I think that's about as close as anyone really can say."

"You have been for years, but people outside of town are starting to notice again." Carol shook her head. "Don't you think it's wonderful?"

"I think it's terrible," Wheeler responded. All three women, even Kate, did a double-take and regarded him with confusion.

"Not 'terrible' as in 'bad,'" he clarified. "'Terrible' as in 'the terrible power of Time.' To be recognized the way I have recently, at my age, is good and bad at the same time, and it's a lot to accept." He shook his head. "So yeah, terrible.

"Anyway, if you were to have a chance to come to the exhibit in Laramie, you could take a look for yourself and see what you think: art, or crap?" Wheeler concluded with a grin.

"I think I know what I'd find," Carol said. "I'd like to go ahead with the first two you showed me, and this black-and-white picture." She shook her head. "Good Lord. The first two will be my present for Steve. This one I'm keeping for now. He may get it later, but only if he's a really good boy."

INTERLUDE: 1945

When Jim had been a young boy, he had once played a coin-operated game outside a department store. As he twisted a metal steering wheel left and right, a small automobile-shaped marker traveled along an image of a road on a scrolling sheet of paper. The more time the little car spent on the road, the higher Jim's score would be in the game.

Now Jim sat in an airplane and watched as actual terrain rolled by beneath him as the trees on the paper scroll had done in the game. A detached part of his mind still analyzed the features below—a bridge here, a railroad track there, an industrial plant off to one side, no military bases in sight—as he had done for the past year and a half. He no longer needed to photograph them, but the reflexes were still in place for now.

He ran a finger around the inside of his collar. It would be a relief to remove the uniform for the last time, but he would need to wear it to make his first appearance at home.

After several hours, the plane veered off of its paper strip and swung out over San Francisco Bay. Jim turned to the uniformed man seated next to him. "Almost there, Gary," he said.

Gary flexed his muscular arms and ran his fingers through his wavy brown hair. His gray eyes seemed happy, but tired. "About time," he answered. "You'd think our triumphant war effort might have turned up a way to make the trip quicker."

"It may yet. Sooner or later, there'll be jet-powered airliners." Jim changed the subject. "How long have you been away?"

"Three years," Gary said. "I was freshly married, but I suffered from a lack of offspring and a surplus of bad timing. It'll be great to see Ruth again."

The plane sank lower and lower over the Bay, and Jim was beginning to wonder whether the pilot had decided to ditch. But just before the wheels touched the water, dry land appeared under the wings. The plane drew its nose back and touched down safely on the runway.

The uniformed passengers on the plane, mostly men with a few women mixed in, clambered out of the plane's side door and down the stairway that had been rolled up against it. They then strode quickly across the tarmac, stretching their legs as they did so, and hastened toward the nearest gate in the nearby fence.

A small crowd of people stood on the far side of the gate. Near the front was a broad-shouldered, olive-skinned woman with long, lustrous, kinky black hair. An enormous grin split her face.

"*Gary!*" she shouted. "Over here!"

Gary grinned back. "Dollface!" He ran to her and they met in a tight embrace.

All around Jim, similar reunions were occurring. Wives, husbands, children, brothers, sisters, others paired off with the people emerging from the gate. Small, chattering clusters of people headed toward the nearby building where the final reunion of the passengers with their grips would, with luck, be accomplished.

Jim stood and surveyed the area around the gate. He looked ahead towards the road that led out of the airport complex, but no civilian vehicle seemed to be on the way in. He followed the crowd toward the building, so that he could grab his own grip and call a taxi.

About an hour later, the taxi deposited him in front of a small flat. He retrieved his grip, paid and tipped the driver, and climbed the stoop. With one hand on the wrought-iron railing, he pressed the doorbell button. After a minute or two, the doorknob rattled and the door opened. Zoë looked at him and smiled.

"Why, Corporal Wheeler! Welcome back!"

"Thank you, Miss Quinlan. It's good to be home."

"Can you stay for a few minutes?"

"That would be nice," Jim said. "Thank you again."

Once Jim was inside, Zoë carefully drew the shades in her front room. She then netted Jim in a quick embrace and greeted him properly with a long kiss.

"Gosh, it's good to see you!" she said. "I've been so worried."

"Well, I wasn't in direct action for very long," Jim said. "After the draft board finally came for me and the Army put me through basic training, I actually showed up only a few months before V-E Day. And it's not like I was in the infantry."

"No," Zoë responded, "but you were up in the air taking reconnaissance photographs. You were a fairly high-profile target for a few months."

"Luckily for me, I wasn't there to do any supporting work for D-Day. But it's all done with now."

Zoë looked Jim up and down. "I do like the look of a man in uniform," she said. "Can you stay, Corporal?"

Jim gave a pained look. “There wasn’t much of a to-do when Johnny came marching home,” he said. He described his arrival at the airport in great detail.

“There is just no excuse for that,” Zoë said. “Estranged or not, you put your ass on the line for us all. The least she could have done is extend common courtesy.” She thought for a moment. “Wait a minute,” she said. “Did you just mention Ruth Markovic?”

“Yeah, actually, I think that was her name. Do you know her?”

Zoë smiled. “She’s a secretary at one of the companies where I do modeling work. Ruth is a bit of a madwoman, but she’s sweet. But we’re straying from the subject. Can you stay?”

Jim shook his head. “You have no idea how much I’d like to. But even if Dora didn’t bother to show up when I landed, she’ll know when it happened. So I’ll need to make an appearance at home. If nothing else, I should check on the kid.”

“All right. But we should figure something out within the next, oh, three days or so.”

“Moved and seconded, Zoë.”

Jim opened his own front door, and heard no answer. He stepped into his foyer, hung up his cap, and leaned his grip against the wall. When he walked into the living room, he found Dora sitting and reading.

“Hello, Dora,” he said, more loudly than necessary.

She looked up from her reading. “Hello, dear,” she said, noncommittally. “How was your flight home?”

"Not bad." Jim felt himself becoming angry, but prevented himself from reacting in the way she clearly wanted. "Long. It felt like we were locked in place for hours on end. It looked like a lot of the families had been waiting for a while, too."

"Families?" Dora asked, confused.

"The families that came out to welcome the soldiers on the plane and get them back home again."

Dora refused to take the bait. "Well, it's good you're back. There are a bunch of things that need your attention."

"Such as what?" Jim asked, still trying to rein himself in.

"Your daughter, first of all," Dora said. "I wonder if she'll even recognize you."

"Well, obviously, I want to see her. Is she here?"

"No, Loretta has her. You'll have to wait until they get back."

"So, not the first order of business, regardless of my preferences, then. What else?"

Dora gave a large, theatrical sigh. "I've had a terrible time with the landlord. You may have noticed that the siding outside is getting very dingy, but he won't do anything about it.

"I'm getting a lot of mail about your business, too. I have no idea what to do about it, so you'll need to take care of it."

"Gladly," Jim said. "I thought about stopping at the office, but I figured I should come here first. In any case, my office keys were here. The extra mail is probably suppliers, and maybe clients, trying to revive normal business now that the war is over."

"Well, that will be helpful."

Finally, Jim reached his limit. "Nothing?" he asked.

"Nothing about what?"

"The whole part about being at war for a year and a half," Jim snapped. "Being a target for the Germans to shoot at. All of that."

"Well," Dora responded, her voice cool, "your letters suggested that you weren't really in that much danger. But in any case, you never had to be on the field, fighting. You were taking pictures, same as you always do."

"It's a little more complicated than that, dear."

"If you say so, I guess." Dora picked up her reading again. "Oh, just to let you know, my bridge nights are still going on. They're on Fridays now, so there's one coming up tomorrow."

"Rest assured," Jim said, "I never forget your bridge nights."

With his return to civilian life, Jim continued to search for new business, and when an assignment documenting agricultural work in the Central Valley became available, he lobbied furiously to get it. For the following three weeks, he spent his Fridays out in the Valley, working as fast and as hard as he could. During the rest of the week, he continued his work for his long-standing clients while he prepared and submitted proofs on the new contract.

By the fourth week, the customer seemed happy. There were a few gaps yet to be filled, but it didn't really mean a day's work. Jim sat at his desk for a few minutes and pondered his plans. Finally, he picked up the receiver on his desk telephone and dialed.

"Hello?"

"Hello, may I speak with Zoë Quinlan?"

"This is she."

"Jim Wheeler here."

The formality dropped away. "Hi, Jim! It's good to hear you. What's up?"

"I've got a short photo shoot in the Valley, but it's a long way to go for a couple of hours of work. So I thought I'd swing into the mountains on the way back and try an outdoor shoot for some of the winter outfits. But with the extra time, that would mean we'd have to get hotel rooms for a night. Would you be interested in a shoot like that?"

"Let me check my book. Just a sec."

Jim counted off the time in his head involuntarily, an unconscious habit triggered by years of darkroom work. Zoë eventually retrieved her receiver and said, "It looks like I'm all clear. And it sounds great. I'll start packing an overnight bag."

"Thank you, Zoë. But you know what?"

"What?"

"That 'just a sec' was actually about three seconds long. So it's a triple sec. Where's the rest of my cocktail?"

There was a short pause. When Zoë's voice returned, she was simultaneously reproachful and giggling. "I'll make you one. I got the recipe from my old friend, Lucretia. You're not going to be doing that the whole time, are you?"

"Not that I'm aware of. But no promises."

Jim packed all his rollfilm gear and as many handheld reflectors as he could find, included his meters and tools, and added his view camera and some loaded film holders for good measure. On Thursday morning, Zoë arrived at his studio. He did not help her out of her coat this time, but led her to his car, and they drove eastward.

Both sessions went extremely smoothly. However, while directing Zoë outdoors in a forest of the Sierra foothills, Jim found himself wishing for extra hands to hold reflectors. An assistant might have helped, but would have disrupted the trip in other ways.

Between shots, Zoë stretched and looked around herself. "What a treat!" she said. "I've always loved coming out here. The air is so wonderful, and it seems like you can see forever!"

Jim looked around. In one direction the forest opened out, and behind it, in regular formation, the rounded ridges of the foothills stretched out as far as he could see, under a serene blue sky with high streaks and occasional cumulus clouds. He glanced to his left, uphill, and saw a good, open clearing where he could set up.

"Does it make you think of anything?" Zoë asked shyly.

"Yeah," Jim said. "It makes me think of my view camera with a 25A over the lens."

"Thanks, Mister Romance."

Jim went to Zoë and kissed her. "My knee-jerk reactions have been with me too long," he said. "I'm sorry about that. I do want to get that shot, though."

Zoë puffed air through her lips in mock disgust.

They found a hotel for the night where they could obtain keys to adjacent rooms. Through some evil supernatural intervention, an accurate guess from the desk clerk, or perhaps a wink of Providence, the rooms turned out to be suite halves, joined by a double door that must be unlocked from the outside on each side to open the doorway. After returning from dinner, Zoë and Jim hung their "do not disturb" signs and opened the door between their rooms.

Late in the evening, it was Jim's turn to sit in bed and watch Zoë sleep. Even with those incredible eyes closed, she was beautiful beyond belief—and yet, it had never been physical beauty that attracted him to her, years before he was willing to admit it. It wasn't sex either, really, although sex there was.

Shortly after she had started modeling for him, Zoë had made Jim feel something he had never had before. Even though they bantered often, he had quickly found himself comfortable, at peace, and cared for in her presence. He had no idea what she had thought about him, and he shook his head to wonder how she had ended up at this pass with him. That first day, she could have easily fought him away, ordered him out, called the police if necessary. Instead, she had taken whatever steps she could to soothe his pain, and she had told him that she loved him.

Why?

In the rare occurrence where a man finds himself the beneficiary of a woman's full, voluntary love, he has no way of processing it. Typically, he will run himself ragged trying to fit logic and reason to it, or in the shadow of years of wandering in the harsh landscape of more common, cynical courtships, he will try to fit this new phenomenon to the map of the world he knows. But Jim was now struggling to deal with it in the manner of a theologian coming to terms with the concept of divine grace. He couldn't explain it, and he couldn't justify it by anything that he had done or refrained from doing. He could simply try to accept it and do his best to be worthy of it.

A thought formed unbidden in Jim's mind. It was a pure thought, but the impure circumstances reduced him to shame nonetheless.

This, Jim said to himself, *must be what an honest marriage feels like.*

In the light of the lamp on his nightstand, he looked down at Zoë. She had drawn the covers over herself and now slept easily. All he could see of her was one smooth, white shoulder, her slender neck, her close-bobbed hair, and one ear. The question he had once asked himself arose again, as it often did:

Why couldn't I have met Zoë first?

He switched off the light at last, and as he nestled close behind Zoë, she stirred slightly. He felt her love and care surround him again, and falling asleep, he descended into the deep, untroubled peace normally enjoyed only by saints and small children.

In the morning they made their way back to the eastern edge of the Central Valley and began to drive across it toward the city. Along the way, Jim slowed the car to look at a small farmstead near the highway. The buildings around the white, two-story farmhouse looked strong, but well worn with years of toil. Around the house and down the long road leading to it, spindly trees were planted. At the outward end of the road, a large FOR SALE sign had been posted.

Jim turned in at the sign and drove slowly toward the farmhouse. Zoë regarded him quizzically.

"I'd like to see if there's anything to shoot here for my personal work," Jim explained. Zoë nodded.

Up close, the compound looked as it had looked from the highway. The clapboard siding on the farmhouse was intact and sturdy, but the paint on it was flaking, and its dull color betrayed the effects of decades of wind and dust. Near the barn, hand tools and other implements were neatly arrayed. Their blades were free of rust but dark with age, and their handles were stripped to bare wood and reshaped by the hands that had wielded them over the decades.

Jim stopped the car, walked to the front door of the farmhouse, and knocked. As Zoë joined him, the door opened.

"Can I help you?"

The woman on the other side of the door was tall and sturdy-looking, but old. Her hair, drawn back in a bun, was nearly as fine as combed cotton and even whiter. Her print dress appeared to have been made at home with yard goods and a pattern, and her face carried an impassive expression bearing witness to a life that prohibited both mastery of and surrender to the forces that shaped it.

"Yes, ma'am," Jim answered her. "You are selling this property?"

"Yes," she said. "Were you interested in buying it?"

"No, I'm a photographer, and I'd like to shoot a few pictures."

The woman seemed confused. "What are the pictures for?" she asked.

"Well, in addition to the work I do for businesses, I take a few photographs here and there to be shown in galleries."

Jim's explanation didn't help. "Would you mind stepping in for a moment?" the woman asked him. "I'd like to understand this, if you have a minute or two."

Shortly afterward, Jim and Zoë had been escorted to a couch, and coffee had been offered and politely refused. "So can you explain this a little further?" the old woman asked.

"Were you aware that photographs are being framed and shown in art exhibits?" Jim asked.

"No," came the reply. "Although there have been a few young fellows like you coming around with cameras for a few years now. I never learned exactly why."

"Well, that's probably a big part of the confusion. People are doing that—creating and showing art photographs—in a few big cities. It's been going on in New York and across Europe for a while now. More recently, a community of artists has set itself up in San Francisco and the East Bay. A few of them are financially independent, but most of us do what artists have always had to do: spend the days doing work that pays the bills, and fitting in the fun stuff where we can." Jim motioned toward Zoë. "We were just driving back from a job taking photographs of clothing for one of the department stores in the city. I came out to find a location for some outside pictures of the outfits, and Miss Quinlan here came with me to wear them and demonstrate them for the camera. We were on our way back when I saw your place here."

"And you think you can take a photograph here and make art out of it? Everything here is worn out and beat up."

Jim asked her patience and thought for a minute. "When you're trying to create a piece of art," he said at last, "you're not looking for the brightest, newest thing. You're looking for people and objects that have something to say. I stopped here because everything here—the house, the barn, the trees, the equipment, and so on—seems to have a story to tell."

"Well, this place certainly does have a story," the woman said. "It's a long one, and sometimes it's been hard to take. But it was a good story, even so. If I could figure out how to keep the farm going, or if I could hire help and still break even, I'd do it. But my husband Tommy passed on two years ago, and none of our kids is able or interested enough to step in. So I'm selling it off and moving in with my second-oldest."

"How long have you lived here?" Zoë asked.

"Fifty years. That's a long time in this business. The weather turns sour, crops go bad, you get bugs, sometimes rodents move in. Other kinds of vermin come out from the bank from time to time. But we didn't care much, Tommy and I."

"Why not?"

A shadow of pain crossed the woman's impassive expression. "We loved each other too much," she said. "I don't think I could have been a farmer's wife for fifty years without that. I certainly couldn't have borne Tommy four children without it." She gave a small, momentary smile. "Or maybe I couldn't have let him live, after all that. But we were so close that we did whatever we could to make it work."

"Maybe I should photograph you, then," Jim said.

"*Absolutely not!* Feel free to take pictures outside, but leave me out of it! Goodness gracious!"

TWELVE

The titanic thunderheads that cruise much of the American West and Midwest are, depending on the viewer's attitude, one of the region's most terrifying experiences or one of its great joys. The enormous, turbulent clouds, laden with rain and hail, arise over mountains to the west and stride eastward with the hauteur of prima donnas and the heavy footsteps of legendary giants.

The environs around San Francisco seldom see such a display.

Jan sat on Wheeler's enclosed porch and watched as one of the behemoths rumbled its way by, whisking the streets clean with wind and water. During these storms, it wasn't any safer to be working around the pipes and sinks in the darkroom than it would be to take a shower or a bath, which no sane resident would attempt at such a time. On the other hand, most of Jan's work was done, so it was no great loss.

Most of the prints for the exhibit had been thoroughly printed, redone as needed, toned, and spotted, although Jan noted smugly that her fastidious darkroom habits had made the spotting stage quick and easy. Only one print had needed to be remade because of the careless twitch of her hand during that last stage. The finished prints had been forwarded to a framing shop to be secured into archival-quality white mats, and then trucked directly from there to Laramie. The University had reported their safe receipt. So Jan had been working intermittently on a few other things, while simultaneously completing a side project of her own.

She had kept in mind the conversation she'd had with Jenny and Greg Myers on the evening of her arrival, and had come to the conclusion that a matted print of one of her own photographs might be a thoughtful thank-you gift. She had chosen one of the images she'd captured in the pastures east of town; personally, she preferred her composition of Roundtop Mountain looming over the cemetery, but she was aware that someone who had relatives buried there might react to it differently than she did. When she discussed the idea with Wheeler, he'd agreed and generously encouraged her to spend time and materials in his darkroom to complete it. But at this point, even that project only needed spotting and matting, and it would be complete as well.

With her routine relaxing, Jan had spent a few hours over the previous week playing tourist. She had even spent an afternoon swimming and sunbathing at the springs, reclining in her silver one-piece bathing suit, oversized sunglasses, and broad-brimmed hat, skimming an escapist novel in the sulfurous air. Here and there, she had stopped to sketch or photograph something that caught her eye.

The storm's gray train swept eastward. Suddenly, the late afternoon sun broke out from behind the storm clouds and reappeared, warm and clear among white streamers near the horizon. Jan took stock of the situation for a moment. She currently had color film in her camera, and cliché though they might be, the sunsets here could be extremely vivid. She left the porch and hurried up the street to the Myers house.

Jan had become familiar with a small rise northeast of town, near the springs, where one could look over the entire town and the mountains far to the west. A few minutes later, she came hurrying up the pathway toward that rise, puffing with exertion. She stopped and looked ahead of her.

At the top of the rise, Kate was standing in the sunlight, trim and unbowed. A small serape-style wrap around her shoulders warded off the chill that the storm had left behind, and as always, her silver concho held her gray hair in a disciplined bundle in the middle of her back. Her arms were crossed in front of her until one of them arose to brush something from her cheek.

Jan proceeded slowly and quietly to avoid interrupting Kate's thoughts. But eventually, alerted to Jan's approach by the crunch of her footsteps on the gravel path, Kate turned around to face her.

"Are you all right?" Jan asked.

"I'm fine, thank you," Kate answered. "Just a lot on my mind."

"Is there anything I can help with?"

Kate hesitated before answering. "Nothing specific," she said at last. "I'm very worried about Jim."

"Why?"

"This show—this exhibit that he has coming up in Laramie, and all of the press attention—it's been a long time coming to him. I want it to go well for him."

"Well, so do I," Jan said. "I've been working like a madwoman to make sure everything goes smoothly —"

Kate cut her off. "That's not it. Oh, I know you've been doing your best, and I appreciate it. But he's had a hard life. I know you haven't seen that side of it, but he has. If this new attention he's getting were to stir too much of that back up, it might hurt him. Maybe I worry too much, I don't know."

"Well, he won't be unsupported, I can tell you that," Jan said. "If nothing else, Fred Lopez is going to meet us there on opening night. He's the guy who sent me out here last year. He'll probably be treating Jim like a rock star. I know he's looking forward to meeting him."

"That will be nice, I suppose. But Jim is going all in on this, and that means he may be ... taking risks." Kate glanced at Jan. "I know of at least one that could come back to bite him on the ass."

Jan was trying to think of something specifically reassuring, but finally proved unable to pin anything down. "I'm sure that it'll be fine, with all of us helping." She paused. "May I ask you something?"

Kate had been gesturing as she spoke. Now she folded her arms again and faced Jan, with the sunset deepening behind her and the faint sounds of distant thunder receding before her. "Go ahead."

Jan took one last pause. "Things between us have been kind of strange," she said at last. "Have I done something to offend you?"

Kate folded her hands before her face, and for a moment, tears seemed to well in her expressive eyes. Then she dropped her arms again.

"You should hurry," she said. "You're going to lose your light."

INTERLUDE: 1946

It was evening. The windows facing the outside world were completely dark, and only the subdued lighting within the gallery itself revealed the artwork within.

Jim had an exhibit opening that evening, and he had spent the past several hours walking around the space, providing quotes and answering questions. At the moment, other than himself and the gallery owner, there were two other people making the rounds. One was a disheveled, rotund man in an ill-fitting suit. The other—a bearded man with a bent nose and an intense, but affable personality—had engaged Jim in a technical debate.

"There isn't any reason for it," he said. "Why let the background fall out of focus?"

"I'm drawing attention the things I want the viewer to see."

"Then why include the other items at all?"

"That's the way our vision works, most of the time," Jim shrugged. "At least I think so. We wade through a visual swamp, and we pick things out."

"If you insist," the bearded man said. "It's a slippery slope, I'll tell you that. The highest standard is that everything in the frame contributes to the overall image, and it's all optimized so that the viewer sees as much as possible. Stepping away from that may not be lazy the way you're doing it, but it will be for the next guy." He shook his head. "From there, it's only a step and a jump till we're making the laziness legitimate by hiding behind some foreign term or other."

Jim chuckled. "Maybe. For myself, I pledge to defocus responsibly."

The bearded man laughed with him. "Well, each to his own. It's good work, Jim. I'm looking forward to seeing what you come up with next."

"Thank you. I appreciate it."

The man stopped briefly to take in some of the other work for sale in the gallery, then left. A couple of minutes later, the other man approached Jim.

"James Wheeler?"

"That's me."

"All this stuff is yours, huh?"

Jim motioned to one side. "Mine is on this side, back to the back wall."

"Yeah, I've looked through it." The man shot a sidelong glance at Jim. "Some nice girlie pictures in the back there, I'll say."

The comment irritated Jim, but it came with the territory. "Well, they're not intended as 'girlie pictures,' for one thing," he said. "It's a long artists' tradition, so many of the photographers practicing right now are continuing it. You could look at Edward Weston, Imogen Cunningham, even Stieglitz did a few. In addition to working in the same theme as the great sculptors and painters, there's an additional challenge for a photographer, and beating it is a mark of skill."

"What's that?"

"Keeping your subject from looking like a freshly-plucked chicken," Jim said. "And in the second place, I wasn't aware that Malcolm was a girlie."

The man pulled briefly at his collar and shrugged. "That's a different matter completely," he said. "You'd better be careful with that sort of thing; it could get you arrested. Not my concern, though." He reached into a coat pocket and retrieved a card, which he handed to Jim.

"You need to come see me as early as possible," he said. "Tomorrow morning would be best. Can you do that?"

Jim turned the card over and puckered his lips.

MICHAEL F. "MICK" CALLAHAN, ESQ.
Personal Injury and Domestic Law

He thought for a moment. "I don't have any meetings or shoots. I'll be there."

Callahan's office was all bare wood and unadorned brick, in the midst of a grimy industrial district. It was about what Jim would have expected from Callahan, by his mannerisms and the way he dressed. Callahan's secretary had ushered Jim to a desk and bade him sit in front of it, and had then left. Jim had been sitting alone at the desk for about twenty minutes, reflecting on the sleepless night he'd just spent and wondering what Callahan was getting at.

Finally Callahan swept in, pulling off an overcoat and hanging it on a nearby coat rack. In the eddies of air that invaded the room, Jim noted the cloying scent of cheap cigars. Callahan placed a manila folder on his side of the desk and sat down.

"Thank you for appearing promptly, Mr. Wheeler," he said. "I'll try to make this as brief and painless as I can. Now, I am being paid to represent your wife, Dorothy MacKinnon Wheeler, in the divorce case for which she has filed the initial petition."

"Divorcing me?" Jim asked. "On what grounds, exactly?"

"Adultery."

"She wants to commit adultery? Well, a divorce would make that difficult. And in any case, it's a bit late for her to be thinking of that."

"This is not a joking matter, Mr. Wheeler," Callahan scowled at him. "You have been observed in various adulterous situations, based on which your wife is filing for divorce." He removed an envelope from the folder and slid it across the desk. "Here is your copy of the petition."

Jim opened the folder and read for a few minutes before he spoke again.

"You think you can make this stick?" he asked at last. "You have no evidence. None."

"Oh, I think we do," Callahan said, reaching back into the folder. "We have photographs. You know all about those, don't you? Good."

Jim fought down a sick feeling as he reviewed the prints in front of him. "This is pretty innocent, and it's easy to explain. I supply photographs to Capwell's for advertising flyers, holiday catalogs, that kind of thing. She works with me regularly on that account—has since I first landed it, actually."

"All right, then." Callahan reached for the bottom of the stack, extracted a print, and set it in front of him. It showed him in a passionate embrace with Zoë, dismissing any excuse of professionalism.

"You know what they say, Mr. Wheeler," Callahan said. "The camera never lies."

Jim jumped out of his seat. "You son of a bitch—"

Callahan rolled his chair back and held up the palm of one hand. "Before you follow through on that," he said, "it would be in your best interest to hear what I have to say.

"First, petitioner has not seen these photographs. She has received a report, but without certain details.

"Second, I want you to look at the first page header on the petition again."

Jim wasn't finished. "What the hell makes you think that these are the only photographs?" he shouted. "Do either of you honestly think that if I thought Dora was cheating on me, I wouldn't take pictures? And I can guarantee you I took them earlier than these."

Callahan quietly repeated himself. "Look at the petition, Mr. Wheeler."

Jim read the first page again. Suddenly he slumped in his chair.

"And there we are." Callahan had a little smile on his face. "I have had your wife agree to certain things in order to ensure your cooperation. If you will refrain from contesting the petition, and if you remain cooperative during the later negotiations, the terms of the decree will remain as you see them. If not, we rewrite it. Do you understand?"

"What about *my* photos?"

"Well, you don't have any way to establish the date and time when you took them."

Jim shook his head and ticked off points on his fingers. "For one thing, the camera was on loan to me. I have the paperwork that I had to fill out when I accepted the loan and when I returned it; it was a total window of about two weeks.

"For another, it is the only batch of thirty-five-millimeter film I have ever shot to this point, so there is no way I could have taken those photographs at any other time.

"Thirdly, I keep processing and printing logs, and I logged that batch just like all my others."

Callahan's expression seemed weary and sad for a moment. It was the first time, then or afterward, that he displayed any humanity in Jim's presence. He shook his head.

"It won't work," he said. "All of that evidence is circumstantial and can be forged."

"You'd have to prove it."

Callahan thought for a moment. "I'm not in the business of giving away free legal advice, Mr. Wheeler," he said, "but I'm going to make an exception in your case.

"I have been engaged to represent your wife in her petition, and I am doing exactly that. Now, you might be able to prove in this case that you have preceding evidence contrary to the claims in the petition. But you would only succeed in that if the third parties were invoked. And if that happens, you won't just be facing me. It will be a team of attorneys. And they will be more influential, and more expensive, than you will be able to afford. Do I make myself clear?"

That evening, Jim sat in his studio office, wincing. In front of him, Zoë was pacing quickly while shouting at the top of her voice, displaying a degree of lexical virtuosity that would have drawn disapproval from the seamen at the Treasure Island navy base nearby. It took a long while for her to wind down.

"That goat-fucking pile of shit!" she shouted. "That pox-ridden, two-bit whore!"

And she slumped into a nearby chair and began to cry.

"Um, *language?*" Jim asked.

"Oh, for Christ's sake, Jim!" Zoë wiped away tears. "That *charming* wife of yours and this goniff she's hired are trying to corner you. You can't let them get away with it."

Jim shook his head. "I may not have a choice," he said.

"Seriously?" Zoë was standing again and gesticulating vigorously. "You have to fight this!"

Wheeler reached into a desk drawer and pulled out his copy of the divorce petition. "I'll tell you what the goniff told me," he said. "Look over the header on the first page. See anything missing?"

Zoë read for a moment. "No."

Jim read aloud: "Filed under the court system of the City and County of San Francisco, State of California: Dorothy Jean MacKinnon Wheeler, petitioner, versus James Wilson Wheeler, respondent."

"So what?"

"The petition does not name a co-respondent."

Zoë knitted her brows for a moment, then looked angry and disgusted. "I'll say it again. *So what?*" she asked.

"Callahan told me that he had 'certain information' he had not shared with Dora," Jim said. "That includes the photographs he obtained, and it also includes the specifics of your identity."

"*I don't care!*" Zoë shouted. "If you need to drag me into this, you drag me in. We'll fight it together."

"I'm not your only client, though, am I?" Jim said quietly.

"Excuse me?"

"You model for many photographers, many companies in town. I know that, and back when our relationship was only professional, I considered myself lucky that I was able to deal with you." Jim smiled. "And obviously, I wouldn't have traded the past three years for anything. I am not ashamed of you in any way. But if you got dragged in, some of your other clients might not be open-minded about it."

"I'm sure it wouldn't be that bad," Zoë reassured him.

"But there's Chambers." Jim said.

Zoë's defiant expression wavered. "Chambers."

"Yep," Jim continued. "I'll give Callahan this much: he's mastered the art of saying a lot without actually admitting anything. Good skill for a lawyer to have, especially an ambulance-chaser like him. He never actually mentioned Chambers by name, but somehow conveyed the following information.

"One: Chambers lined him up for Dora.

"Two: dragging Chambers into the trial automatically drags you in as well.

"Three: if Chambers gets involved, his legal staff gets involved. As you probably know, he has a lot of them, and they're expensive. Anyone who gets in his way gets ruined. Therefore, both of us would be ruined."

Zoë had calmed down by now. "How do you know he won't ruin us anyway?"

"You may remember that I have pictures of him with Dora," Jim said. "Callahan is of the impression that those pictures, and the audit trail I have on how and when they were created, could be discredited. I'm not so sure. But I'm a lot more certain that Chambers doesn't want them to come out in public in any way.

"Meanwhile, he's still working what mischief he can." Jim reached into his desk again. "This came by courier this afternoon. Effective immediately, Chambers Industries terminates all professional dealings with the Wheeler Studio. Check attached covers balance payable in order to close accounts." He put the envelope down. "Depending on what terms the judge orders, I could be in serious trouble. I can only hope that Chambers does the honorable thing and marries Dora."

Zoë laughed bitterly. "The honorable thing? The man is a slumlord and a slave driver. He has no honor in him. And there's something else."

"What?"

"There's a certain type of man," Zoë said, "who screws women to make himself feel powerful. He takes pleasure in the pain he can inflict on others. He humiliates the women and emasculates their husbands. He doesn't care about them at all. And I can tell you point-blank that if I had ever thought your mind worked that way, that first day in my flat would have ended up with you in a police car, nursing some embarrassing wounds.

"But Chambers *is* that kind of man. As soon as the ink is dry on the divorce decree, he'll drop Dora like yesterday's garbage, because that's all she'll be to him."

"And that's that, I guess," Jim said quietly. "I could lose everything."

"Not everything," Zoë shook her head sadly. "Never everything."

"How can you say that? I don't even know how I'm going to keep going if things get really bad. How can I possibly make it worthwhile for you?"

Zoë gave Jim a sad little smile. "Don't you even dare," she said, kissing him. "We'll struggle through it. Where are you staying tonight?"

"I've got a cot that I need to set up in the back room," Jim said. "It's back there with all of the boxes of stuff that Dora wasn't interested in; they were waiting on the porch when I tried to go home."

"Harlot," Zoë said. "Well, you can come home with me tonight, and we'll tell everyone you slept on the couch. It's not like we have to be that secret anymore; we'll just keep up appearances for now. It'll be a relief."

THIRTEEN

Jan stood in Wheeler's office, as she had the previous year. But the environment was completely changed. She was not at all uncomfortable, and nothing seemed mysterious or threatening.

Wheeler, as always, was hard to read—not deliberately evasive, as he had been the first time she had seen him, but still very reserved. The two of them had worked together for most of the summer, but he still kept many things about himself private and did not venture much information. There was one other issue that both of them had circumvented throughout the entire summer, and Jan was still unsure whether she should confront it.

"All done," Wheeler said with evident satisfaction. "All the pieces are either in my truck or in Laramie. If we've missed anything, it's not anything important. The world will survive, and so will the exhibit. You have your print for the Myerses?"

"Right here," Jan motioned toward the frame under her arm.

"May I?" Wheeler asked.

"Of course."

Wheeler laid the frame flat on his desktop, where two of the track lights converged. He examined it at an angle, first from the left, then from the right. Then he fished in a desk drawer and brought out a large magnifying loupe, which he used to examine a couple of spots. Finally, he put the loupe away again and brought the picture back to Jan.

"Well done, very well done," he said. "Particularly with such a subtle subject. The subtle ones are like making a good cheesecake. If you leave lumps in, people will *know*." He handed the photograph back, looked around himself, and patted his pockets. "Let me see … I'm missing something … Oh, right!"

Wheeler ducked behind his desk again and opened the center drawer, rummaging briefly to ensure that both sets of keys he had loaned to Jan were safely back in his possession. He then emerged and spoke again.

"We will be meeting in Laramie, right?" he asked.

"Right," Jan said.

"So we'll say our farewells at the end of the evening, then. But before we go, I did want to say that I think you've done excellent work and shown a lot of talent. If you decide to concentrate on photography in your upper-class years and afterwards, I think you could go far. Thank you for your help."

Wheeler extended his right hand. Jan, moved by his words, decided to cross the remaining boundary and embraced him.

"Thank you for everything, Grand-dad," she said.

But when she drew back, Wheeler's face looked troubled. He motioned her toward the front door.

"I'm sorry, but I've got to get on the road," he said. "We've both got a long way to go and not much time to get there. Don't be late!"

After Wheeler locked the door, started his truck, and sped off, Jan hurried up the street to the Myers house. She did a quick check of her car to make sure all her possessions were there, then climbed the porch steps and rang the doorbell.

Jenny Myers opened the door. "Oh, it's just you, Jan!" she said. "Why didn't you just come in?"

"I'm all moved out and cleaned up," Jan said. "So I don't live here anymore, and that means I have to ring the doorbell just like door-to-door salesmen and everybody else."

Jenny waved her argument away. "Pffft. Don't be silly."

"Listen, I have to get on the road to Laramie, but I have something here for you. I've been working on this while I've been here."

Jan handed the picture to Jenny, who looked it over carefully. "This is lovely, dear. Thank you very much."

"Thank *you* for all of your hospitality," Jan countered. "I made sure to tell Greg last night because I knew he'd be at work by now. But could you please say goodbye again for me?"

"Oh, of course," Jenny said. "Hug for the road?"

They embraced and exchanged a few final pleasantries, and then Jan drove away. Before leaving town, she stopped to buy something to drink on the way, and before she got back into her car, she took a deep breath and a final look around.

The midmorning air was warm and even drier than it was when she had arrived, if that was possible. The sagebrush on the hills and bluffs had reached its full growth and now spread its scent far and wide. Jan remembered her dismissive attitude the first time she had entered the town, and marveled that although nothing had changed, she hesitated to leave. Nevertheless, being on a tight schedule, she took one extra deep breath, got into her car, and drove away.

Across the long, not-quite-empty spaces, Jan drove to Laramie at the best speed she could manage, then checked in at her hotel. She quickly unpacked and touched up the one dress she had brought with her, showered, dressed, did her hair and makeup, and hurried to the University.

As she approached the gallery, she saw a printed sign:

J.W. WHEELER
A Testament of the Inner West
Opening Tonight

Not far inside the door, Wheeler was standing in a light brown western suit, complete with bolo tie. Next to him, Kate stood in a bright red western blouse, pressed slacks, a small squash-blossom necklace, and one of her ever-present concho hair ties. Wheeler waved at her; Kate nodded as usual. Just past them was a familiar face Jan hadn't seen in months.

"Hey, Fred!" Jan called.

Fred Lopez spun around. "Jan! You've been busy this summer, I see."

"No kidding. Have you met Jim?"

"Yeah, we've been introduced and exchanged a few words. Seems like a reasonable guy. But he's had plenty of people to keep him busy: University people, potential buyers, other folks."

"Have you had much of a chance to look around?"

"Oh, yeah." Fred waved the question off. "Jim says that the hometown contingent had to drive down here from Thermopolis this morning. I flew into Cheyenne last night. So I've been here longer than any of you."

"So, what do you think of the work?" Jan asked.

"There's a lot of wonderful stuff in here," Fred said. "People are going to be really excited. Now, Jim said that you printed the core images, but he worked with consultants on the color landscapes and the figure work."

"He just said that he needed to enlarge from eight-by-ten," Jan said. "I never heard what the subject matter was."

"Well, Jim says that those six prints—five women, one man—represents his entire oeuvre in the nude figure genre. But his emphasis on human detail really shines in those images. It's amazing; he should make a killing on the prints, or he should hold on to them until people come to their senses. But that's not the interesting thing."

"What is, then?"

Fred grinned. "One of his models was my Great Aunt Inés."

Jan did a double-take. "Really? That's kind of an odd coincidence."

"Right," said Fred. "I mean, Aunt Inés was always gorgeous, so it's not surprising that she should turn up modeling for someone. And they were in the Bay Area at the same time. But … small world, certainly." He paused. "Actually, Sylvia Fordyce is in there too. She was Aunt Inés's roommate for about forty years straight, so it's not surprising that one of them would recommend the other one."

"Roommate," Jan said. "For forty years."

Fred shrugged and spread his hands. "Big Catholic family, mid-sixties. One did not ask."

Just then, Jan saw a familiar mass of loose, strawberry blonde hair drift by. "Excuse me a moment, Fred. *Carol!*"

Carol Bradford turned around. "Oh, hi, Jan!"

"Came all the way down, huh?"

"Well, after the work Jim did for me this summer, I thought I should come see for myself."

"And what do you think now?"

Carol shook her head. "It's mind-boggling. He's been doing all of this work for almost fifty years, and no one ever knew about him. He was taking school pictures in a little town for all these years, when he was capable of so much."

Jan saw tears forming in Carol's eyes. "Easy there, easy. You'll mess up your mascara. Do you need a tissue?"

"No, thanks," Carol said. "I can hold it together. I *think*. I haven't looked at everything yet."

"Me either. There are some things in here that I didn't print, and I need to make sure and give them a good, close look."

Jan wandered the walls of the exhibit. First, she checked up on the pieces she had printed, paying special attention to her old friends. There was the Devil's Tower image—Bear Lodge, she corrected herself. Nearby hung her personal favorite, the half of a ruined farmhouse with the endless prairie behind it. A group of middle-aged people she didn't know was clustered around one print; Jan wondered idly whether it was the print she'd made of *Barnyard*.

Jan moved to the minuscule arrangement of color images. Most of these were studies of banded stone, but Jim had thrown in two prints of the flowstone terraces next to the springs in Thermopolis. She had no idea how he'd managed it, but these pieces had the same sculptural look that graced his black-and-white images. She would need to read up on that dye-transfer process.

After an hour or so of evaluating photographs and chatting with other guests, Jan decided it was time to look through the side gallery behind the PORTRAITS AND FIGURES sign. As she stepped through the doorway, she noticed that the light here was more subdued; track lighting accented the pictures hanging here.

Jan stepped slowly past the portraits, checking on them as she had done in the main exhibit; she had printed most of these as well. The more recent ones showed a distinctive combination of smooth, soft lighting and razor-sharp detail that suggested Wheeler had invited the subjects to his solar studio. But at the far end of the passage hung the six oversized frames containing all the nude figure studies that Wheeler claimed ever to have completed in his lifetime. For each of these, Jan read the title before studying the image.

The first one was titled *Sylvia, 1941,* so Jan assumed it must be Sylvia Fordyce, the "roommate" of Fred's Great Aunt Inés. She looked up at the giant frame to see a tall, thin, exceedingly white woman with platinum blonde hair, standing ramrod straight with her hands clasped behind her. With her long, thin face and her stern expression, she seemed almost wraith-like. Jan moved on.

The next image was *Malcolm, 1943,* the sole male study in the group. The young man was clearly a bodybuilder; the surface of his torso was laid out in disciplined phalanxes of muscle, and his overall outline was a design exercise in diagonal lines. He had turned his face away from the camera to emphasize his strong jawline, and the leg toward the camera was extended forward to honor the taboo of the time regarding male genitalia in images of this kind. Of course, Fred had made sure she knew all about Robert Mapplethorpe, but that had been thirty years or so after this.

Next came *Diana, 1943*. Nothing could be seen of Diana other than her hair and her back, but these were carefully arranged to form one smooth, sinuous curve from top to bottom—an exercise in minimalism that Jan appreciated.

After that was *Inés, 1941*. Jan took a long look at Fred's great aunt. He wasn't kidding. She was a curvaceous knockout, with long, wavy, dark hair and huge eyelashes. Jan found herself wondering what on earth Sylvia had to look stern about. She studied the image for a minute, then moved on.

The next image was *Laura, 1942.* Of all the figure studies she had seen so far, this was easily Jan's favorite. Wheeler had posed Laura in a pose closed off by arms and shoulders, and then cropped the negative in camera to cut off just below her elbows—and Jan immediately understood why. In the finished print, the lines and curves, and the gradients of Laura's flawless dark skin, led the viewer's eye inevitably to Laura's most compelling feature: her beautiful, dramatic, slightly sorrowful face. Jan left the image slowly to read the title card for the last figure study.

It read *Zoë, 1942*.

Jan felt the punch-in-the-stomach sensation again. Zoë? The only specific thing the lawyer had told her about the woman that had caused her grandmother to sue for divorce was her first name, and that name had been Zoë. And 1942? The date was one year *before* the picture she'd found in Wheeler's files, showing her grandmother with Frank Chambers.

Wheeler had lied to her. Just like he'd lied to her mother and grandmother before her.

In her anger and pain, Jan slowly raised her eyes to confront the image of her grandfather's mistress. But as soon as she had done so, she felt another punch. The pain threatened to overwhelm her.

In the oversized frame before her, Zoë reclined on an indeterminate shape covered in finely woven, medium-gray canvas. By whatever technical tricks he had had available to him in the forties, Wheeler had rendered the woman into the texture of flawless sculptural marble, the only exceptions being painted nails on her hands and feet, and those other details that were darker than her overall skin tone.

Jan looked at the woman's face. It was beautiful, of course, with a slight smile, but she found her attention drawn to the eyes.

Zoë's eyes, which had attracted Jan's attention even as they had once attracted Wheeler's, were her most compelling feature. They were dark, dramatic, compelling, and slightly mischievous.

And utterly unmistakable.

When Jan emerged from the side gallery, she saw Wheeler with Kate and Fred. She strode over to them immediately.

Fred asked, "Jan, are you all right?" Jan ignored him and stared Wheeler in the eyes.

"You lied to me," she said.

"What do you mean, Jan?" Wheeler asked, his voice tired.

"It says 1942 in there. *1942*. That's a year early."

Kate—formally, Zoë Katharine Quinlan—spoke up. "Jan, please be patient," she said. "You don't have all the details yet."

"I know what I need to know," Jan shouted. "And I don't need to hear *anything* from *you!*" Tears spilling down her face, she spun around and strode angrily out of the gallery.

Fred ran after her. "Jan, wait!" he said. "You're missing something. *Jan!*"

Five minutes later, he was back. "I couldn't get her to turn around," he said. "At this point, based on what she's learned, she should understand what happened. But she's not seeing it."

"I tried to warn you," Kate told Wheeler, shaking her head sadly. "I told you she was going to be trouble."

At her hotel, Jan told the desk clerk to refuse all calls. And the first thing the next morning, she paid for her room, slammed her car door, and headed west on the Interstate without ever looking back.

INTERLUDE: 1942

"Good afternoon, Zoë. Come in, please." Jim locked the front door, took Zoë's coat, and escorted her back to the studio. It was a warm, sunny afternoon, and the painful days were still far in the future. At this point, to all appearances, Zoë and Jim were trusted professional colleagues and nothing more.

Zoë looked around. In the center of the floor was an indeterminate piece of furniture, a couch or chaise, draped in dull, neutral gray fabric. A dark fabric backdrop lay behind it, and surrounding it at fairly close range were several scoop lights, some modified with barndoors or scrims as normal. Jim's big view camera stood between and slightly behind two of the lights. The shade was drawn over the studio's single outside window and a second fabric backdrop stood in front of it.

"All right," Zoë said cheerfully. "So what am I modeling today?"

"Excuse me?" Jim looked around himself in horror. This was not a day for a misunderstanding.

But Zoë laughed. "Don't worry. I know what the plan is."

Jim took a deep breath and attempted to dispense with his previous rush of panic. "I must ask: are you still all right with this session?"

"Yes."

"And the terms are appropriate?"

Zoë smiled. "Yes."

Jim gave a small, nervous shrug. "Well then, the changing room is in the usual place."

Five minutes later, Zoë appeared in a bathrobe. "What sort of pose did you have in mind?" she asked.

Jim moved to the draped piece of furniture. "I was thinking of a semi-reclining position. Hopefully, the drape isn't too bad."

"It's kind of dull, don't you think?"

"Well, I don't want it to grab the viewer's attention. I like the background to fade out; you know me."

"All right, then." Zoë turned her back, removed the bathrobe, and handed it to Jim. She then stepped to where she was to pose. Turning around slowly and with great ceremony—a gesture that made Jim smile despite his professional detachment—she sat down and arranged herself.

"How's this?" she asked.

Jim looked and knitted his brow. "Try scooting down a little and extending your right leg out. That looks better. How is it for you?"

Zoë grimaced. "I don't know how long I can hold out this way, Jim. I feel strung up like a suspension bridge. Isn't that showing in my neck?"

Jim looked again. "You're right, it is. Well, how far up do you need to sit to get rid of that tension?"

Zoë scrunched back a few inches. "How does that work?"

"I think that'll do fine. Your feet are about where they need to be. Can you put your upper torso a bit toward me and drape your left arm along the top edge of the chaise? Thanks. Right hand should be hanging half open and resting just inside your right hip."

"Do you need to reach over and position things?"

"Thank you for the offer, but let's do this by the book for now," Jim said. "In a bit ... about an inch more ... then relax that hand. Perfect!"

Grabbing a loupe, Jim ducked under his focusing cloth. He made a few final adjustments, then emerged and picked up a film holder. "Before we continue," he said, "I'm going to ask you one last time. Are you still comfortable with proceeding?"

Zoë looked slightly exasperated for a moment. "Yes, I am, for the third time. If it makes you feel any better, I've sat for life-drawing classes many times for a few extra bucks."

She thought for a moment. "I remember one time, there were two of us sitting, a matched set, boy and girl. The boy was a young man named Malcolm. Very handsome. Built better than Johnny Weissmuller. I'd known him since high school, and in those days I'd had an *enormous* crush on him. But for the life of me, I couldn't get his attention—and I can tell you, I tried everything short of semaphores and signal flares.

"Well, in that class the two of us sat there for forty-five minutes, perched on those damned stools—this is much more comfortable, by the way, and thank you—but when it was over, I made sure to be especially dramatic about standing up and stretching. Then I walked over to where Malcolm was and chatted with him, catching up on our lives." Zoë shook her head. "Still not married, no girlfriend ... and no reaction! *None!*" She chuckled. "Looking back, I may have missed something about old Malcolm."

"Hmm." Jim thought a moment. "Do you think you could find him now? I haven't tried this with a man yet, and I think I probably should."

"I'll see."

"Thanks. But one thing to keep in mind is that you will be more recognizable in a photograph than you would be in a sketch." Jim thought for a moment. "Actually, if I was the one doing the sketch, no one would know *what* you were. That's why I went into photography to begin with. But seriously, you will be a bit more visible than you're used to."

"I think we have that covered in the release," Zoë told him. "If you just show them in tasteful exhibits, that'll be all right. Please don't run them in the *Chronicle,* though."

"Thanks again. Are the lights okay? Not too hot?"

"No, actually. I think they had naked women in mind when they designed them, the reprobates. I'm just nice and warm."

"Well, good," Jim said. "Goosebumps are a curse we don't want right now. Your right hand has slipped a bit. Could you bring it back up? Face neutral but not mad … good. Hold still …"

The two worked in the studio for about half an hour, trying different arrangements while exchanging small talk. Every so often they paused and Zoë set herself in position while Jim took another exposure.

"So how are things going for you at home these days, Jim? Still good?" When Jim's face fell, she corrected herself. "I'm sorry. I didn't mean to pry."

"'S all right," he said. "But no, things aren't still good. I was expecting some disruption when Clara was born, but I'd hoped that when she started sleeping on a normal schedule and eating solid food, the tension level would go down. No such luck. We're back to feeling like barbed wire should be strung across the living room."

Zoë raised an eyebrow, but Jim refused the bait. "Of course, Dora's taken up with her bridge ladies again. That was a priority for her as soon as possible. The marriage, not so much."

"You ever think about getting out?"

Jim looked appalled. "What happens to Clara then?" he asked. "None of this is *her* fault, is it?"

"No, I suppose not."

They worked through a few additional shots before Zoë spoke again. "You know," she said slowly, "it's almost gotten to the point where some people would take the completely cynical route."

"What do you mean?"

"Well, if they can't fix it and they can't step out, they start something on the side."

Jim looked out from behind the camera, shocked. He then recovered his balance and attempted to disarm the conversation.

"Why, Miss Quinlan, this is so sudden," he said, grinning.

For a tiny instant, Zoë's face fell slack in amazement. Then, almost at once, she set it into lines of annoyance. "*Honestly!*" she exclaimed, jumping to her feet and stomping toward the camera. "You can't even leave a simple expression of concern where it is without making some sort of proposition out of it?"

"Honest, Zoë, I thought it was just our usual ..."

She cut his sentence short. "I mean, really ... do I *look* like I'm trying to seduce you?"

Jim shrugged and spread his hands. Zoë stared at him for a second, not comprehending. Then suddenly she looked down at herself, shot him an evil glare, and grabbed the bathrobe from the chair next to him.

Fifteen minutes later, with the misunderstanding largely patched over, Jim watched Zoë as she walked down the sidewalk, more briskly than normal, back straight, shoulders back. He honestly had not intended anything more than their typical studio repartee, and so her response had caught him off guard. He acknowledged to himself that Zoë must certainly be more ill at ease under today's shooting conditions than she was willing to admit. Under the highly unlikely event that he had another such session with her, he would need to be more circumspect in his comments, or perhaps avoid them entirely.

And there was one other thing that bothered him. In that flash of an instant between his ill-placed joke and her display of anger, the expression in those gorgeous, expressive eyes hadn't simply been shock. It looked sad, almost painful. If it had happened with anyone else, Jim felt certain that he would not have seen it; her eyes had betrayed her.

But try as he might, Jim could not figure out what that expression had meant.

FOURTEEN

Jan drove through the long spaces, through southern Wyoming and Utah and Nevada, as though fleeing a demon. Upon her return home, she met briefly with her mother, who commiserated with her about her experience.

"I'm so sorry things went so bad, hon," she said, embracing Jan. "But I tried to warn you. I told you he was going to be trouble."

Jan put the experience behind her as well as she could and quickly ventured into her junior year of college. About two weeks into the fall semester, one of her professors flagged her down as she was leaving the classroom.

"Excuse me, Janice," the professor said, "but I have a message for you."

"Okay?"

"Fred Lopez asked me to let me know that he wanted you to stop by his office."

Jan's lips tightened. "I don't want to talk to him."

"Is there a disciplinary problem, Jan? Something that should be reported?"

"What?" Realizing that her professor was checking for abuse or harassment, she responded quickly. "Oh, no, no. Certainly not. This summer, he and I attended an event that didn't go well for me. I don't know whether he wants to console me or cross-examine me, but I don't need to find out."

"Very well, Jan," the professor said. "If that's the way you feel about it, I'll let him know."

It took another two weeks for Fred to find her. He saw her walking between classes and flagged her down.

"Jan! Jan, please wait a minute!"

She stopped, face tight and angry. Fred reached her within a few seconds.

"Jan, I understand that you're upset. But can we please talk for a minute?"

There was a long pause. "Go ahead," she said at last.

"I just wanted to raise the possibility that Jim Wheeler may have been telling you the truth the whole time."

"You're kidding, right?"

"No. Look, before you go," Fred gestured quickly with his hands, "just answer me two questions."

Jan sighed impatiently. "Oh, all right."

"You've had to do life-drawing lessons, haven't you? In your classes?"

"Yes."

"Were you romantically involved with the models there?"

"No," Jan answered, irritated. "Where are you going with this?"

"A photographer is like any other artist in those situations. Some of them can't keep the business and personal stuff separate. Some can. For me, the one time I tried it, I spent ten minutes arguing politics with my model before I realized she hadn't put her clothes back on yet. I was oblivious, and she was getting pretty cold."

"So?"

"So there's a scenario in which, yeah, Jim had asked Kate to sit for him, and he was involved with her, but not at the same time. See?"

"Oh, come on, Fred. How likely is that?"

"It's one of the only circumstances I know of where possession of a photograph of someone without benefit of clothing is not necessarily *prima facie* evidence of a sexual relationship. A nudist colony would be the only other one I can think of. But Jim told me that they became involved a little over a year after that session took place."

"You believe him?" Jan asked. "It's awfully convenient, isn't it?"

"Yeah, it is. But stranger things have happened." Fred hesitated. "Listen, Jim asked me to deliver a message, no further strings attached. He just wanted me to say that he was sorry for the way things turned out."

"I don't care," Jan snapped. "To have my nose rubbed in it without warning like that, and then I come out and she's right there next to him."

"'Right there next to him,'" Fred repeated. "*Forty years later.* Doesn't that count for something?"

"No. She helped destroy my grandparents' marriage, Fred. Whose side are you on, anyway?"

Fred hesitated. "At the risk of sounding insanely pompous … I'm on the side of the truth. It comes with the territory of being an art teacher. With something like Jim's situation, that can be hard to figure out, but I'm doing the best I can. I also care about you, by the way. I don't want you to throw a big part of your life away without good reason."

"Me?" Jan asked. "I'm not even in any of your classes this semester. What do you care about me?"

"You're obviously not a teacher." Fred shook his head. "You have been my student, and sometimes that's enough, even though you won't be my student again."

"Why not?"

"That was the other thing I needed to tell you about. I've got a new job, starting the first of the year. I'll be at the University of Wyoming."

"Why in the hell would you be moving out there?" Jan asked.

"It was a couple of different things coming together at the same time," Fred explained. "They had a vacant instructor's position in their art department. At the same time, in conjunction with setting up his exhibit, Jim apparently asked them to provide a home for his archives, and they agreed. So we all made a deal. I'm going out to set up the Wheeler Archives, make sure they're maintained and protected, for the next couple of years. Meanwhile, I'll also be teaching the same sort of classes I've been teaching here."

Jan had calmed down a little. She shook her head and gave him a rueful smile. "So you are in cahoots with him, after all."

"Not for this conversation. I just want to make sure that you have all the information before you make your final decision about all this. Jim says his attitude all along has been that you and your mom shouldn't have had to be held accountable for things you couldn't have changed. He was genuinely disappointed to see you leave the way you did."

"And Zoë—excuse me, Kate?"

Fred shrugged. "Less generous. I'm not sure why." He started away. "Listen," he said, "think about it, would you? Don't cut him off completely without being very careful about your reasons."

Jan paused. "I'll think about it."

"Don't take too long," Fred said. "You never know how long you've got."

INTERLUDE: 1985

Something awakened Zoë in the morning twilight. Outside, beyond the thin curtains, the first red rays of dawn amplified the color of the stony hilltops in the distance. On and around the stones lay a thin layer of dry snow.

She was in the little bedroom at the top of the stairs in Jim's studio, and she had fallen asleep with one arm around Jim, as she usually did. This morning, though, something felt wrong—heavy, cold.

Zoë withdrew her arm and sat up in the bed. She leaned over and placed a hand across Jim's forehead. Then she moved it to his neck.

"Don't you dare," she said softly. "Don't you even dare."

Zoë bowed her head and began to weep.

FIFTEEN

Jan reorganized her remaining courses to place special emphasis on graphic design, then settled down and got to work. To the extent that she could, she put the events of the previous summer out of her mind.

On a rainy afternoon in the last week of February, she arrived back at her apartment following the day's classes. She set down her books and her purse on the kitchen table, then flipped through the envelopes that had arrived in the mail, stopping when she reached one from the University of Wyoming.

The envelope contained no note, nor any handwriting on the scrap of newspaper within it. Jan unfolded the paper and read its contents.

J.W. Wheeler, Photographic Artist, Dead at 67

James Wilson Wheeler, a local photographer who became widely known late in his life because of artwork he had created in his youth, died of natural causes February 7 at his home in Thermopolis. He was 67 years old.

After Wheeler had worked humbly for decades, photographing at least two generations in Thermopolis, he suddenly attracted wider attention when the burgeoning market for photographic artwork took an interest in prints he had shown and sold in San Francisco in the 1940s. The additional publicity led to a retrospective exhibit sponsored by the University of Wyoming, featuring work from his California period and newer images he had stockpiled in his later years. A selection of these photographs is expected to be published as a coffee-table book later this year.

A private funeral has been held.

Jan sat for a few minutes, deep in thought, with the clipping in her hands. She felt sad that Wheeler was gone, even a little wounded that she hadn't been invited to the funeral. But of course, she reminded herself, that was to be expected given the way things had turned out the previous summer. Her instincts still told her that he had lied to her … and yet, a small voice underneath them asked whether she was completely sure of that. Should she have at least given him a chance to tell his side of the story, if he had been willing to do so? Didn't she even slightly regret that if there was a misunderstanding, she could never correct it?

Once again, she put the thoughts aside and returned to her studies. But two days later, there was another envelope. The return address on this one identified its sender as Raymond Girard, Attorney at Law, Thermopolis, Wyoming.

Dear Ms. Gibson:

I have been entrusted with the execution of the last will and testament of the late James Wilson Wheeler. As one of the terms of said will, he bequeathed to you certain personal effects which I must now hand over into your possession. If it is impossible or inconvenient for you to receive these bequests at the address shown above, please contact me by mail, telephone, or fax in order to negotiate terms of shipment.

Please note that some of the items are fragile. If it is necessary to ship them to you, I will endeavor to protect them in any way I can, but I will not accept responsibility for damage in transit.

Best regards,

Raymond H. Girard, Esq.

This made no sense at all. Why exclude Jan from the funeral and then include her in the will? After a moment, she understood the reason: Wheeler would have prepared the will himself, in advance, but others had arranged the funeral on short notice—and those others would have included Kate, as well as other people she had alienated at her departure.

The small voice had continued to nag at her. It was now asking whether, even if she had not been welcome at the funeral, it wasn't worth a trip to pay her last respects. While she was there, she could pick up the items Wheeler had left her and avoid the risks associated with shipping them, whatever they were. The following morning, she called Girard and made arrangements with her instructors.

A week later, Jan found herself driving into Thermopolis once again. She had recognized Girard's address as being in the old downtown area, and after turning off the highway at the appropriate intersection, she pulled up in front of his office.

As she stepped out of her car, she noticed a familiar mass of strawberry-blonde hair a few doors away. The woman underneath the hair was walking briskly away from her, wrapped in a coat that looked unusually bulky. Or was she pregnant? Jan reflected that Carol's wedding had been six months earlier, so there had been ample opportunity even by the book.

"Hey, *Carol!*" she called out, but Carol did not break stride. "Carol?" Still no change. Carol reached a door in a nearby storefront and stepped quickly inside. With slight disappointment, Jan located the door to Girard's office and followed suit.

Raymond Girard turned out to be a middle-aged man with close-cropped, grizzled hair, thick horn-rimmed glasses, and neatly pressed clothes. His gravelly voice seemed never to shift in pitch, volume, or rhythm, and his impassive expression gave testimony to the too many stories he had heard and the too many fools he had had to suffer.

"Thank you for coming, Ms. Gibson," he said, motioning her to a chair adjoining his desk. From a spot against the wall, next to a stack of boxes, he retrieved a bulky carrying case and placed it on the desktop.

"Mr. Wheeler left you two separate items in his will," he said. "This is the first one, and I'll need to do some digging to find the other one." He slid a form toward her. "Please sign the form to acknowledge receipt of the first item." Jan signed the form and slid it back.

When Jan opened the case, tears welled up in her eyes. The case contained one of the new rollfilm cameras that Wheeler had bought with his grant money the previous year, along with three lenses and a few smaller devices. Over all of it a note had been laid:

Dear Janice,

If you are receiving this package, it means two things:

First, I am dead, and therefore I have no more need of the contents.

Second, the contents are still in new enough condition to be of use to you, and therefore I have passed on sooner than I would have preferred.

If you decide to pursue photography as a career, this equipment may be helpful. I believe you have real talent, and if you exercise it, it will grow.

Please understand that I took great pleasure in the time we spent working together, and in your company. I am sorry for the way things worked out in the end. I believe that if you knew the whole story, you might have understood a little better. But it was unreasonable to ask you to absorb in three months what the rest of us have been soaking up for decades.

Best regards,

J.W. Wheeler

"Are you all right, young lady?" Girard asked, turning from his search through the boxes that had been next to the case.

"Yeah, I'll be okay," Jan said with a sniffle. "Just out of curiosity, were there any real surprises in the will?"

"Nothing major," Girard said as he resumed his shuffling through the boxes. "Parts of it are confidential, of course."

"Sorry, I didn't mean to pry."

"No harm done. His last instructions were a little bit silly. Maybe it was his mechanism for dealing with consideration of his pending demise. He specified only a simple grave, with two words of text added to his headstone, and a small, private funeral. Then he said that he should be left above ground for three days, and that someone should tickle his feet just to make sure he was dead. If he didn't respond, he said, they could continue with the burial."

Jan snickered a little through her tears.

"There's a claim period in which people who came to him for work can claim the original filmstock for that work, subject to certain conditions. At the end of the claim period, the remainder of his files go to his archives.

"And there were a few sealed envelopes. One of them was for young Mrs. Paulson; she came in just before you did."

"Yeah," Jan said, "I saw her leaving when I came in."

"And one of the others ..." Girard peered into a box. "... is yours. Ah, here you go." He placed a sealed manila envelope on the desktop, along with another receipt form. "Please sign for this one as well. Sorry, they're two separate paragraphs in the will."

Jan signed the second form, then opened the envelope. It contained a stack of accounting sheets showing years of checks: alimony, child support, and miscellaneous payments. On top of the stack was another note.

Dear Janice,

I beg your pardon in advance for the contents of this envelope. However, because of some of the matters we discussed the day we first met, I felt that it might be worth passing these records to you and your mother in order to clarify any points of confusion.

Regarding the other items in the envelope, I leave it to your best judgment whether to discuss them with your mother.

Regards,

J.W. Wheeler

Jan turned the envelope on end and shook it. Two yellowed slips of paper fell onto the desktop. Jan looked at them for a moment and shrugged. "I don't get it," she said. "What are they?"

Girard picked the slips up. He then slid his glasses down his nose and peered over them for a better look. "Lab reports, looks like," he said. "Both from the same hospital on the same day—July seventeenth, 1947."

Jan thought for a moment. "That sounds like my mom's bad accident," she said. "Mom always said she slid down a broken metal slide on a playground when she was six years old and sliced the side of her leg open. She lost a lot of blood. But she said that her dad never bothered to show up at the hospital."

"Well, either your mom is wrong, or this is a different incident," Girard said. "One of them is marked three-thirty P.M., the other is at about five o'clock." He paused and read a little more. "They look like blood typing reports, so he was there, and trying to find out whether he could give your mom some of his blood."

"Oh, for God's sake!" Jan exclaimed, now irritated again.

"What?" Girard asked.

"Every time I ask a question, the story changes. What happens next? Does it turn out that my grandparents were never really married to begin with? Or what, exactly?" She calmed herself. "Sorry," she said.

Girard turned his attention back to the slips of paper. "Let's see ..." he said. "James Wilson Wheeler, blood type AB, negative. Pretty rare. Good thing *he* never got into an accident."

He switched to the other slip. "Clara Jean Wheeler ..." He stopped abruptly, pursed his lips, and let out a long breath.

"What is it?" Jan asked.

Girard shot her a sideways glance and continued. "Clara Jean Wheeler, blood type O, positive."

"So he wasn't able to give her any blood, is that it?"

"Partially," Girard said, tossing the slips back onto the desktop next to the envelope. "But they're not just medically incompatible, they're genetically incompatible."

"What are you saying?"

"A type-AB-negative man cannot father an O-positive child."

INTERLUDE: 1947

Jim strode quickly down the hospital corridor. Just as he was about to turn right and enter the room where he'd been told Clara was, he saw a doctor emerge.

He appeared in the doorway just long enough for Dora to see a flash of him walking past. She turned from her watch over the little girl and regarded him with a cold glare that the lines around her eyes amplified.

"Doctor!"

"Yes, what is it?" the doctor asked, annoyed at the interruption.

"I'm Jim Wheeler—Clara's father. How is she?"

"Ah. Walk with me, please. Time's a-wasting." The two of them sped back down the corridor, nearly as quickly as Jim had come in. "Your daughter tried to play on a metal slide that had broken loose along some of its welds. That left a metal edge exposed. She's got a bad laceration on her left leg. We've put sutures in, but she's lost a lot of blood. I'm going to place a call to the blood bank now, so that they can rush some over in the right type. We're low here, unfortunately."

"I'll gladly give some, if that would help."

"Thank you, Mr. Wheeler," the doctor said briskly. "Blood type matching can be tricky, even with close relatives. So I'll place the call to the blood bank and send a nurse to get a sample from you, both. Please wait here. Excuse me."

Jim sat in the waiting room the doctor had indicated. About five minutes later, the nurse appeared: perhaps twenty-five years old, tiny, with yellow-blonde hair and bright blue eyes, a canary of a woman. "Mr. Wheeler?" she asked.

"Yes, that's me," Jim answered.

"If you'll follow me, sir, we'll take some blood and get it to the lab to see if little Clara can use it. This way, please."

Jim sat in a tiny room for five additional minutes while a phlebotomist applied a tourniquet to his upper arm and drew a syringeful of blood. Afterward, with an adhesive bandage inside the crook of that arm, Wheeler was escorted back to the waiting room.

He sat on the edge of the chair, tapping his fingers nervously. He wanted to get up and go reassure Clara, but he knew that if he was a close enough match, he could do her more good where he was. He would have to give her his apologies after the crisis was over, he told himself, tiptoeing mentally around the possibility that it might not end well if the doctor's efforts weren't quick enough.

After another fifteen minutes that seemed endless, the nurse reappeared. "Mr. Wheeler?"

"Yes, miss?"

"Good news, sir."

"You can use me?" Jim asked with relief. "Excellent. Let's get started. Where do I go?"

"Oh, no, sir," said the nurse. "The truck from the blood bank got here in record time, and we've started Clara on the first unit. She's already much better.

"Unfortunately, we couldn't have used your blood. Too many mismatched factors," the nurse continued. "That's why it was so important that the blood bank people got here when they did. They must have broken a dozen speed limits, honestly."

"Well, as long as Clara's all right," Jim said.

"Of course, sir," the nurse assured him. "This must be one of the toughest things to deal with about adopting a child, but as long as you love her just the same …"

Jim gave a double-take. "Adopting a child?" he asked, confused. "What are you talking about?"

The nurse looked at him, blinking her blue eyes uncertainly, for about five seconds. Those eyes then widened, and she put one hand over her mouth.

"Oh, my God!" she said. "I'm sorry, sir …" She abruptly turned tail and flitted from the room.

Jim stood up and retrieved his jacket so that he could go see Clara. He was heading out of the waiting room when he heard the doctor behind him.

"Mr. Wheeler?"

Jim turned back. "Oh, doctor," he said. "Thank you for your patience earlier, and obviously for getting Clara all squared away."

"Mr. Wheeler, can we talk for a moment?"

The doctor motioned him back to the seat he had occupied, and sat down opposite him. He took out a pad of paper, a pencil, and two small yellow slips, which he presented to Jim. He then spent about five minutes drawing boxes, dividing those boxes into sets of four smaller boxes, and writing combinations of letters in them as he spoke.

Finally, the doctor finished his lecture. "Are you okay, Mr. Wheeler?" he asked.

Wheeler was not okay. His heart raced and his mind grabbed for something to use as an anchor. Dora had called him as soon as the ambulance had reached the hospital, and from his new, smaller, cheaper live-in office in San Leandro, he had broken speed limits himself getting here. And now, none of it was worth a damn.

His mind went back to the days right after he had signed that first deal with Chambers. Everything had seemed so much better between him and Dora in those days, but it had all been misdirection, sleight-of-hand. Just like the "bridge nights" and all the rest.

"Yeah, I'm fine," Wheeler said at last.

"Okay," said the doctor. "I apologize for the way Nurse Schmidt dropped this on you. It was highly unprofessional. She will be reprimanded."

"Don't go too hard on her, Doctor. She's just out of nursing school, isn't she?"

"As a matter of fact, yes."

"Well, she's still learning, then. She's got a lot to take care of." Jim changed the subject. "And Clara is out of danger?"

"Yes, she'll be fine. She'll be out raising hell again in a month or two. But hopefully she'll be a bit more careful."

"All right," Jim said. "Thanks again."

He stepped out into the corridor, then slowly turned to the left and shuffled away. He knew Dora had seen him come in, but he couldn't risk facing her where Clara could see them.

That poor kid, he thought to himself. *What kind of life is she going to have?*

As Jim opened the hospital door and left, Clara shifted painfully in her hospital bed.

"Shhh," Dora said. "Be careful, honey, and try not to move too much."

"It hurts, Mama," Clara complained.

"I know, dear. But you'll need to take care of it so that it can heal quickly. When the nurse comes back in, I'll ask if there's anything else she can give you. Try to be as comfortable as you can."

The two of them sat in silence for a minute or two before Clara spoke again.

"Mama?"

"Yes?"

"Did you call Daddy?"

"Yes, I did."

"Where is he?"

"I don't know, honey," Dora said. "Maybe he's not coming."

SIXTEEN

Jan sat in her car, in the cold, dry air and thin sunlight of the fading Wyoming winter. The temperature in the car dropped gradually; she huddled in her seat and attempted to hide her nose, duck-like, inside her jacket.

No relation.

She was not his granddaughter. Her mother was not his daughter. And yet, he had paid the terms of his divorce, moved all the way here so that he could continue to do so without giving up his profession.

Why?

When she had come looking for him, he had encouraged her to continue believing in the lie.

Why?

And the following summer, when he saw an opportunity to mend fences, he invited her out and treated her as his own.

Why?

What was the point? Had he entertained some sort of bizarre revenge fantasy, of leaving Chambers with a bastard grandchild who was actually his in spirit?

And was she actually the descendant of Frank Fucking Chambers—the dissolute, decrepit, shambling financial tyrant whom every social change activist group at her university held as its most cherished target? She found herself wishing fervently that the genetics companies down the Peninsula and out in the East Bay were further along in their research; it would be worth money for her to disprove that link, if it was possible.

But then, they might also confirm it.

Jan noticed a shadow in the blinds covering the storefront window in front of her. That would be Girard or his assistant, wondering why she hadn't moved—or whether she needed medical help, perhaps. She started her car, reminded herself to check thoroughly behind her in order to avoid flattening someone in her continuing emotional shock, and backed into the street. As she drove away, she could see a sheriff's department vehicle about a block away, so she continued to pay close attention to her driving.

Where to go? Where could she finish sorting all of this out?

Without full awareness of what she was doing, she drove through back streets until she arrived at Wheeler's studio. The property had already changed hands; Wheeler's business sign was gone from the front yard, and someone appeared to be in the midst of remodeling the front room that he had used as his office.

Jan looked behind the house. The greenhouse was half gone; the new owners were dismantling it. Jan began to shiver, and tears ran down her cheeks. She drove away again, followed in about thirty seconds by the sheriff's car.

There was only one remaining thing that Jan could think to do. She returned to the highway and drove toward the north end of town. When she reached the gift shop, she pulled over and got out of her car. But the old signs and decorations were gone. All that remained was a single sign bearing the words FOR SALE and a telephone number.

Jan walked back and forth in front of the building, peeking through the windows, trying to find some clue about where Kate might be.

"She's gone," came a man's voice from behind her.

Jan turned quickly to see the sheriff's car standing in place with its engine running. Its driver, a tall, muscular, familiar young man, stood next to it, a scowl of disapproval on his face.

"Steve Paulson?" Jan asked. The man nodded.

"I was just at Mr. Girard's office ..."

"I know," Steve said. "He called the station, said he was worried about you. The jokers I work with thought it would be good to send *me* out."

"I was hoping I could talk to Kate," Jan continued.

"She's not coming back."

"Do you know where she went?"

Steve shook his head. "She had family in the Midwest somewhere. After Jim died, she decided to go stay with them. Too many painful memories here, so I can't say I blame her.

"I don't know any more than that," he concluded. "And if I did, I wouldn't tell you."

Jan felt herself starting to cry again, but stopped herself short. It became apparent to her now that Carol hadn't failed to hear her earlier, she had simply refused to speak to her. She calmed herself until she could risk speaking again.

"I still need to pay my respects, at least," she said. "Can you tell me where Jim is buried?"

Steve's expression softened slightly. "I can drive you there, if you want."

"Thank you," Jan said. "I'd appreciate it."

As Steve put his car into gear, he began to speak. “It was Kate who called us first,” he said. “About nine A.M. on the seventh. She said that she’d tried to contact him, but he hadn’t answered his phone or his doorbell, and she was worried.” He shook his head and smiled. “Thing was, most people in town—and just about everyone at the office—knew something was up between the two of them. And when we broke in and found him there, all we did was to check that there was no foul play. We made sure that the coroner confirmed it later, of course. We knew she was lying to us; she knew he was dead because she was sleeping there at the time.” He smiled again. “Typical citizens aren’t good at removing their own traces, even when they try. And Kate was careful, but she missed a few things that an officer would notice.

“I also found a pair of fuzzy slippers tucked way under the bed,” Steve continued. “I don’t know if she’d worn them recently or not, but I’m pretty sure they would have looked stupid on Jim.”

Jan laughed a little, through her tears.

The car made its way up a little rise, toward a scene Jan knew well: the simple, unadorned cemetery at the foot of Roundtop Mountain. Steve continued talking as he found a suitable parking spot and stopped the car.

“After Jim died, Kate sat down with Carol and me and told us the whole story.”

“The *whole* story?” Jan asked. “His business, the marriage, the affair, everything?”

Steve nodded. “None of us knew that Kate had been a model for years and years. Not that it took that much imagination, really. Carol always says that she’d kill to look that good when she gets to that age. Kate stayed in the Bay Area for years after Jim moved out, posing for photo shoots, sometimes even being an extra in movies. But she told us that when they started sticking her behind baby carriages whenever she reported to a shoot, she knew it was time to go. She said she'd be damned if she was going to hang around until she was putting on white wigs and posing with plates of cookies. So then she followed Jim out here."

"Did Kate ever mention why Jim never mentioned any of this to me?"

"She wasn't sure. She told us that he used to say something about not visiting on the children the sins of their parents."

Jan fished in her pocket and retrieved the two yellow slips of paper. She handed them to Steve. "Did she tell you about this?" Jan asked. "Did she even know?"

Steve looked at the slips and handed them back. "Yes on both counts," he said. "How long have you known?"

Jan's voice was suddenly very small. "An hour," she said. "Maybe a little more."

"Well, come on." Steve opened his door. "It's right over here."

JAMES WILSON WHEELER
JULY 15, 1917—FEBRUARY 7, 1985
Fiat Lux

The ground over the grave was still disturbed and raw. The thin, cold wind whistled around the squat bulk of the mesa, through the spindly trees nearby, and over the cemetery, scattering dust as it went. Jan walked to the graveside, adjacent to the headstone, and knelt down.

"It's dirty already," she said, tenderly brushing the accumulated grit and dry grass away with her hand. She knelt, silent, for five minutes or more, before she spoke again.

"Reciprocity failure," she said at last.

Steve looked down, confused. "*What?*"

"It was something he taught me about, last summer," Jan said. "It was a photographer's way of saying that two things that are equal to the same thing aren't necessarily equal to one another."

Steve shrugged. "Okay."

"They told me that he'd cheated on my grandma, and that was true," Jan continued. "They said that Grandma divorced him over it, and that was true. Mom said she couldn't get an extra buck out of him to save her life, and that was true, too, at least from her point of view. A lot of things were true. But they weren't right."

Her voice wavered at the end. "And the one thing I wanted to be right … wasn't true."

And she dropped to her haunches, abandoned all pretense, and cried.

Eventually she stood up, wished Wheeler peace, and said goodbye. Steve returned her to the gift shop. As she got out of his car, however, something locked into place within her. The stories, the reports, the rumors, the colorless facts, and the accusations all broke apart and fell away. And at that moment, Jan straightened her back, put out her shoulders, and tossed back her hair.

"To hell with it," she said to herself. "It doesn't matter. They were all in pain. The only thing that matters is what caused the pain."

She turned back toward the sheriff's car. "Hey, Steve?"

"Yeah?"

"Would you do me a huge favor?"

"Okay."

"Please talk to Carol for me," Jan said. "Tell her that for whatever it's worth, I didn't understand and I can't explain how sorry I am. Would you do that?"

"Sure." Steve nodded, then thought for a moment. "Or we could go find her and you could tell her yourself."

"No, I can't stay," Jan said. "I have to get home."

She looked around the rocky hills and then up north, toward the billowing steam clouds emerging from the springs.

"I have some work to do," she said at last.

Steve waved, put his car into gear, and left.

And after one last deep breath and one final look around, Jan drove southward, down the long canyon and away, never to return.

EPILOGUE

Sunlight was everywhere.

In a nondescript bedroom in the American Midwest, the white curtains glowed with it, and the linens on the small bed shone with warmth. Among them a motionless figure reclined. In the absence of the vibrant spirit that had filled it for so many years, it seemed unreasonably small.

"Auntie Zo?"

A woman's voice called from beyond a door. She called again:

"Auntie Zo, are you all right?"

The door opened, and the owner of the voice strode in quickly: middle-aged, with white streaks threaded through her dark brown hair and lines of care graven into her face. She put a hand to the face of the woman in the bed, then grasped the wrist reclining on the bedspread. With her other hand, she covered her mouth as her tears began to flow.

A magazine lay open and unregarded in the middle of the bedspread, cold winter sunlight strewn across it. An article showed on the page that the figure in the bed had last seen.

Today charges were brought against Chambers Group, the large and powerful international conglomerate, accusing the firm of fraud related to environmental and labor policy violations that have recently come to light, and the systematic steps the firm has taken to conceal them from the federal government. Investigators revealed and detailed the extent of the Chambers Group's deceit after graphic-designer-turned-photojournalist Janice Gibson published her now famous photo-essay, which first brought the firm's practices to the public's attention.

And on a wide stretch of meadowland in the Inner West, the blades of wild grass jittered rigidly in a thin, cold breeze. Under the hard blue sky, their life force retreated under the crumbly, dry ground, cloistering itself deep in the roots to wait out the advancing siege. Around and among them were tiny seeds, primed to bring forth the wildflowers in the coming spring, as they did every year. Dry snow blew through the endless stretch of brown and tan. In the distance, a haze of fresh white haloed mute red terraces.

It was November, and the world was at rest.

www.ingramcontent.com/pod-product-compliance
Lightning Source LLC
Chambersburg PA
CBHW030117260626
47156CB00008B/2691

* 9 7 8 0 6 9 2 0 9 8 0 6 6 *